STAR TREK®

S T A R G A Z E R
MAKER

Michael Jan Friedman

Based upon
Star Trek: The Next Generation®
created by Gene Roddenberry

POCKET BOOKS
New York London Toronto Sydney

An *Original* Publication of POCKET BOOKS

POCKET BOOKS, a division of Simon & Schuster, Inc.
1230 Avenue of the Americas, New York, NY 10020

Copyright © 2004 by Paramount Pictures. All Rights Reserved.

STAR TREK is a Registered Trademark of Paramount Pictures.

This book is published by Pocket Books, a division of Simon & Schuster, Inc., under exclusive license from Paramount Pictures.

ISBN: 0-7434-4858-8

First Pocket Books printing September 2004

10   9

POCK
Simo

Cover

Manu

For i   es,
please   -6798
or bus

For Debbie and Stu, who understand

STARGAZER
MAKER

Chapter One

ANDREAS NIKOLAS HAD RUN into his share of alien species. He had attended the Academy with them, worked alongside them on starships, eaten with them, slept with them, laughed with them, and risked his life with them.

But he had never encountered anyone like the personage who towered before him in an otherwise empty corridor of the Yridian cargo hauler *Iktoj'ni.*

This alien was taller than Nikolas by half a meter and remarkably thick-chested beneath his coarse, dark tunic, giving the impression of enormous strength— though he was quite clearly padded elsewhere with a surfeit of flaccid flesh. His oblong head was bald except for a long, lank circlet of dark hair, and his mouth was little more than a gash in his face.

But his most distinctive feature by far was his eyes.

They glowed a dazzling silver beneath the overhanging ledge of his brow, fixing Nikolas where he stood.

"I am glad you are awake," said the behemoth, his voice a hair-raising jangle of stones.

It echoed off the cone-shaped mineral deposits that hung from the ceiling and rose from the floor—because it wasn't quite true that Nikolas and the alien were alone in the duranium-sheathed passageway. There weren't any other sentients there, but there was an abundant collection of orange- and blue-veined stalagmites and stalactites—the kind that seemed to belong in an underground cavern, not in the corridor of an Yridian cargo hauler.

And if that weren't disconcerting enough, the projections were growing before Nikolas's eyes, lengthening and adding girth with the help of the mineral-bearing water streaming down their sides.

Where was the water coming from? He didn't know. The *Iktoj'ni* wasn't supposed to have any water supply. Its crew washed with the help of sonic emitters and got their drinking water from replicators, the same as their food.

So why were there crystalline threads descending the smooth, shiny surface of the stalactites? And how could mineral deposits have gotten so robust in the short time Nikolas had been stretched out on a lower deck?

Awake, the alien had said. But *was* he awake?

He had lost consciousness sometime during the attack on the *Iktoj'ni.* And though he appeared to have woken up, bruised and limping and lacerated but alive, it was tempting to believe he was still asleep—because otherwise, how could he explain the madness to which he had woken?

Several days earlier, Starfleet had warned the cargo hauler about a wave of unidentified aggressors boasting formidable weaponry. But it hadn't said anything about ship's corridors turning into subterranean caves.

"After all," the behemoth continued, in the same discordant voice, "you are going to be a big help to me." He smiled, exposing a rampart of thick, blunt teeth as his mouth stretched from one side of his face to the other. "A *big* help."

Nikolas didn't like the sound of the remark. "What do you mean?" he asked, his voice sounding strange even to his own ears.

It gave him a moment's pause. Had he suffered some damage in the attack after all, beyond the cut over his eye and the painful stiffness in his limbs?

The alien didn't answer Nikolas's unspoken question—not out loud, anyway. But as the silver orbs in his eye sockets glowed brighter, Nikolas heard something in his brain.

My doing, said the monster, in a small, harsh whisper. *All my doing.*

A telepath . . . ? Nikolas thought.

And the alien's smile spread even wider, though the human wouldn't have believed it possible. He seemed to be taking pleasure in Nikolas's discomfort.

But it's not enough, the colossus breathed in Nikolas's mind. *I need more.*

Suddenly, the human felt a shiver rise from the

depths of his being and take hold of his entire body—a shiver of shock and helplessness, because the alien wasn't just speaking inside his head anymore. He was dredging up memories.

The death-scream of a thousand finger-sized quadrupeds on Mercker V. The bitter stench of tortured metal after a grisly shuttlecraft crash. The glint of sunlight off an old woman's hair on a fertile moon of Samito III . . .

The alien wasn't gentle about it, either. He stalked about Nikolas's mind without conscience or compunction, probing and prodding, not caring what he damaged in the process.

Semi-sentient life-forms slithering under the surface of an inland sea. The feel of scales on the naked thigh of his Heiren lover. The bite of homemade ouzo on his tongue, setting fire to his throat and then his brain . . .

The intruder thrust himself into every fold and crevice of the human's experience, sampling and rejecting, violating privacies great and small. Nothing stopped him, nothing was off-limits.

Nikolas couldn't stand the feeling of invasion. It filled him with such revulsion, such self-loathing, that he wanted to escape his own skin. Concentrating with all his might, he tried to expel the alien from his brain.

But he couldn't. It was like trying to wrestle an enraged *mugato.* And just as Nikolas realized how powerless he was against the invasion, how utterly overmatched, the alien began to thrust even deeper into his consciousness.

Nikolas could have given in to it. He could have allowed his captor to run roughshod and saved himself even greater discomfort. But he didn't. He continued to struggle.

It was a futile gesture. The alien was simply too strong, too determined. So Nikolas wasn't surprised when he felt himself submerged in a raving, synapse-shattering wave of pain . . . or when he felt his consciousness slip away again into the depths of a slow, black sea . . .

Jean-Luc Picard gazed across his desk at the strapping, blue-skinned officer who had come to see him. He knew exactly what his visitor wanted.

Still, he allowed Vigo to broach the matter his own way, in his own time. The Pandrilite had earned that privilege with his valor, his dedication, and his unswerving loyalty.

"You'll recall what I told you about Pandril," said Vigo. "What Ejanix told me before he died."

"I do," said the captain.

Ejanix had been Vigo's mentor and close friend. Prior to his untimely death, he had insisted that their homeworld—a supposed utopia in which all classes of society were supposed to thrive—was riddled with tyranny and injustice. Vigo hadn't believed it possible—not at first. But the more he had considered the matter, the more he felt it was his duty to determine the truth.

Of course, Ejanix had become a revolutionary over the years, someone who had come to tolerate the use of force in the name of social change. Vigo didn't condone that approach—he had already said as much. But it didn't mean that he could dismiss Ejanix and his compatriots out of hand.

If it turned out that they had a point, Vigo wanted those in the upper caste to be made aware of the problem. And as a member of the upper caste himself, he felt he was uniquely suited to the work of informing them.

Picard sat back in his chair. "You wish to take advantage of that leave we spoke of?"

"Yes," said Vigo. "For the reasons we discussed."

The captain nodded. "I understand. And I will not stand in your way. If you feel you must go, I will make the necessary arrangements immediately."

Vigo looked grateful. "Thank you, sir."

Picard dismissed the need for gratitude with a wave of his hand. Vigo was a mainstay of his crew. The captain just wished he could do more for him.

"Dismissed," he told Vigo. "And good luck."

The lieutenant nodded, then got up and left. As he exited the room, Picard took a good look at his weapons officer, knowing he might never see him again.

It wasn't that he thought Vigo would prefer to remain on his homeworld. He believed that, in time, the Pandrilite would want to return to Starfleet, and to the *Stargazer* in particular.

Picard just wasn't certain that he would still be commanding the *Stargazer* when Vigo came back.

He caught a glimpse of his reflection in the screen

of his computer monitor—that of a fellow with prominent cheekbones, a strong, cleft chin, and inquisitive brown eyes. A *young* man, to be sure. And yet, he was already developing worry lines above the bridge of his nose.

But then, he had more worries than most men his age.

In a week's time, he was slated to report to Starbase 59. Shortly after he arrived, he would attend a formal hearing, the subject of which would be his actions as commanding officer of the *Stargazer,* and his future in Starfleet.

There would be three admirals present to hear his case. One was McAteer, his superior, and the man who had arranged the hearing in the first place. Another was Mehdi, who had made Picard a captain and given him command of the *Stargazer.*

If all went as expected, McAteer would try to tear Picard down while Mehdi did his best to defend Picard's decisions. One against one, an even contest— or it would have been, if McAteer and Mehdi had been the only combatants.

But the third juror—and there had to be a third one, lest the contest end in a draw—was Admiral Caber, whose son had been unceremoniously kicked off the *Stargazer* for what Picard had believed were good reasons.

The younger Caber had seen the matter otherwise. And at the time of his departure, he had threatened to use his father's influence in Starfleet to get even with Picard.

The Cabers' chance to do that was close at hand. All the admiral had to do was side with McAteer and Picard would be abruptly stripped of his command—not to mention his rank.

So when the captain wondered if he and Vigo would ever have a chance to serve together again, it wasn't an idle question. It was a very real concern.

Frowning, he ignored his reflection and focused on the list of Starfleet advisories on his monitor screen. He might not be a captain much longer, but for the time being he would continue to do his job.

Nikolas woke to the feeling of something cold and wet against his cheek. Lifting his head, he saw that a puddle had gathered beneath his face in a trough formed by three stout, still-growing stalagmites.

No, he thought, correcting himself. They weren't just stalagmites anymore. They had connected with the stalactites growing above them, creating complete, hourglass-shaped columns. In fact, the corridor was lousy with them in both directions.

But the alien was gone.

Nikolas felt a wave of relief. What the invader had done to him . . . he never wanted to experience it again.

He hadn't known that a telepath could pillage someone's mind that way. But then, the only telepaths he had known were a couple of doe-eyed Indrotti on Risa, and they had obviously been more interested in his body than his mind.

He wished he were back on Risa at that very

moment. He wished, in fact, that he were anywhere but on an Yridian cargo hauler inexplicably turned into an underground chamber.

He touched his fingers to the puddle in which he had been lying and tasted it. It was water, all right. But where the devil was it coming from? And how was it manufacturing cones of accumulated mineral matter so quickly?

Nikolas remembered what the alien had said to him: *My doing. All my doing.*

But that was ridiculous. No one had the power to create this kind of environment on a spacegoing vessel . . . did they?

Examining the mineral column closest to him, Nikolas saw that it was hard and surprisingly smooth to the touch. And it had to have come from *somewhere*.

He had read stories of seemingly magical beings in the logs of the early starship captains—a teenager who had been brought up by powerful aliens, a mysterious humanoid named Trelane, even the ancient Greek god Apollo. But no one like them had turned up in the last fifty years, and there was speculation that they had never really existed in the first place.

There has to be an explanation, he told himself. *It can't be the alien who's doing this. Not on his own.*

Then he remembered the other thing the behemoth had said: *But it's not enough. I need more.*

What the hell did he mean by *that?* More mineral accumulations? What good could they possibly do him?

Nikolas would eventually have to find out. But first,

he wanted to know what had happened to his crewmates—his friend Ed Locklear and all the others. If they were lying somewhere all broken up, Nikolas doubted they would get any assistance from the alien.

The question was where to look first. Fortunately, he didn't have to dwell very long on the answer. He had been on his way to the bridge when he encountered the alien. It was still the most promising destination he could think of.

Making his way through the forest of blue and orange columns, he found a turbolift and waited until the doors slid aside for him. Then he entered the compartment, punched the necessary code into the control panel, and watched the doors close again.

The last time Nikolas had attempted a ride in the lift, the compartment had stopped partway to the bridge level and the doors had opened, apparently on their own. And that was when he had encountered the alien.

A coincidence? It didn't seem like one. But he wasn't ready to believe that the invader was responsible. It was one thing to violate a mind and another to stop a moving turbolift.

In any case, the lift didn't stop this time. It kept going, moving in determined fashion through the ship, until it reached its appointed destination.

When the doors parted, giving Nikolas access to the corridor, he got out and looked around—and found the same conditions that had prevailed two decks below. Cone-shaped projections coming from both the ceiling and the deck beneath his feet, each of them waxing larger right before his eyes.

But that wasn't all he saw. Partway to the bridge, nearly hidden by a bend in the corridor, a pair of boots was lying on the deck—and Nikolas had a feeling they weren't empty.

Negotiating a path through the field of stalagmites, he got near enough to confirm it—there were legs attached to the boots, and a body attached to the legs. But it wasn't yet clear to him whose it was. The only thing that *was* clear to him was that the body was no longer alive. It was too thin and too pale, and it was lying at too awkward an angle—the kind no humanoid could have adopted and survived.

Feeling a lump in his throat, Nikolas advanced a little farther and saw that it was Redonna, the Dedderac who had piloted the ship. She was tough as duranium, as reliable as they came—and she had made a pass at him the night before the attack.

"You see," she had said, her voice low and lusty, *"I've had my eye on you since the minute you beamed aboard. It gets lonely on a cargo hauler. But there are ways to relieve the loneliness . . ."*

Nikolas swore under his breath.

In life, Redonna's skin had been a series of wild black stripes on a white background. In death, the stripes seemed to have faded, leaving her looking pale and washed out. But that wasn't the worst change in her appearance. Her cheeks had sunken, her eyes had retreated deep into their sockets, and the skin around her mouth had become dry and cracked.

It was as if she had had the life drained from her. It didn't make sense, but that was how it appeared.

When she came on to Nikolas the other night, he had rebuffed her. But part of him had been tempted to go along with the idea. She was, after all, an attractive female.

Or had been.

Nikolas knelt on his bruised and battered knees and brushed his fingertips against Redonna's face. Her flesh felt so cold, so *terribly* cold, that it was hard to imagine it had ever been any other way.

He had barely known her, but he felt that he should do something for her—that it was up to him to mark her passing somehow. What could he do?

Putting the problem aside for the moment, he decided to walk on, in the hope that he might find another survivor. But as he negotiated the first bend in the corridor, all he came across was another corpse.

It was Murata, one of the engineers. He was human, but he looked a lot like Redonna now, his skin contracted around his bones so tightly it was painful to look at him. And like Redonna, he was well past the point where he might have benefited from Nikolas's help.

Around the next bend, Nikolas found three more bodies. Sadly, he identified them in his head. Happy-go-lucky Jetraka, who had just celebrated his hundred and seventh birthday. Kroda the Tellarite, who had been so indignant when one of the other crewmen jostled him in a corridor. Yellowstone, the chess player. All of them sucked dry, like ancient mummies.

But not Nikolas. *Why not?* he asked himself. What bizarre providence had spared his miserable life when all these others had been sacrificed?

Moments later, he came to the doors that gave admittance to the bridge. As he approached them, they whispered open for him, revealing the scene beyond.

The *Iktoj'ni*'s command center was a good deal smaller than that of a Federation starship. It held only three stations—the captain's, the helm officer's, and the navigator's. There was no room to accommodate a communications officer, an engineer, a sciences chief, or a weapons officer.

Still, the bridge had been a busy place, with personnel coming and going all the time. *Usually*, Nikolas added silently.

Not now, though. Those who had come and would have gone were stretched unmoving among the beginnings of blue and orange stalagmites, their handheld computer devices spilled from their grasps. And those ensconced in the three control stations were slumped forward in them, as if they had gone to sleep and had yet to wake up.

But they won't be doing that, Nikolas thought with a sinking feeling. *Not if they've fallen afoul of the same thing that killed Redonna and the others.*

Just to be sure, he approached Captain Rejjerin, who had ignored Starfleet's warning for the sake of making her ship's delivery date. A Vobilite, she had ruddy, mottled skin and tusks that protruded from the corners of her mouth. Nikolas felt her neck for a pulse. There wasn't any, and her skin was icy to the touch.

Just like the others, he thought. There wasn't a mark on her, but she had clearly been dead for some time.

Is everyone *dead?* he thought.

And how in blazes had they died? What kind of weapon could rob a person of their life's energy that way?

Then he saw something else—the configuration of stars on the large, octagonal viewscreen that covered the bridge's forward bulkhead. It was wrong, it seemed to him, different from what it should have been.

Someone else might not have noticed. But Nikolas had sometimes served as a navigator on the bridges of Federation starships, guiding them through this part of space. He knew what the screen should have looked like.

Gently, he removed the helm officer from his station, which was wet with the drip from a stalactite directly above it, and laid him on the floor. Having already begun to stiffen, the fellow lay grotesquely on his side, with his head laid across his outthrust arms.

Nikolas forced himself to ignore the helmsman's corpse and concentrate instead on the helm controls. They weren't all that different from those he had manipulated in his Starfleet training sessions.

A small screen in the upper right corner showed him their course as a red line on a black-and-yellow grid. Sure enough, it had changed since the attack.

The *Iktoj'ni* wasn't heading for the trading world called Djillika any longer. She was on a course that would take her into the portion of space occupied by the Ubarrak.

And she was doing so at full speed. Nikolas felt his throat go dry.

Ubarrak territory was the last sector he or any other

Federation citizen would be advised to visit. Though the Federation wasn't officially at war with the Ubarrak, the possibility of an armed conflict was always implicit in their strained and often hostile relations.

Slipping behind the helm console, Nikolas slowed the cargo hauler to a crawl. Then he punched in a new heading—one that would take the vessel back to the heart of Federation space—and engaged the thrusters.

When he looked up at the viewscreen, he saw the stars scrolling from one side to the other, reflecting his course change. *Much better,* he thought.

Suddenly, Nikolas heard footfalls. Heavy ones, too heavy to belong to one of his crewmates.

Swiveling in his seat, he saw the alien looming over him, his eyes glowing feverishly. But he wasn't returning the human's scrutiny. His head was tilted to one side, as if he were listening to something Nikolas couldn't hear.

What's going on? Nikolas wondered. Giving in to an impulse, he turned back to the viewscreen—and saw that the stars had begun moving back the other way again. Glancing at his helm console, he noticed that his course change had been nullified. Once again, they were heading for Ubarrak territory.

What the hell . . . ?

Behind him, the alien stood gazing at the screen. He looked pleased with what he saw.

"We have resumed course," he said in that strange, discordant voice of his.

A part of Nikolas couldn't believe the invader had reset the helm controls without touching an instrument panel, or that he could stop a moving turbolift or make a cavern out of a ship's corridor. But another part of him was starting to believe that it was possible—and that if the alien *had* done those things, he could drain the life from Nikolas's comrades as well.

It seemed crazy. And yet, the evidence was starting to pile up. The invader possessed abilities far beyond anything Nikolas had ever seen.

But that didn't mean the alien was a match for the Ubarrak. Not all by himself, in a lightly armed cargo vessel.

"You don't want to go where we're headed," Nikolas said reasonably. "The Ubarrak don't like outsiders."

"I know," said the alien, his voice every bit as harsh and ringing as before. "I noticed that when I reached into your mind to find a destination."

Ignoring Nikolas, he turned to Rejjerin and raised a four-fingered hand—and the captain ascended from her station. With a horizontal gesture, the alien slid her through the air to another part of the bridge. Then he dropped his hand, and Rejjerin plummeted to the deck with a thud.

With the captain's chair vacated, the alien settled his bulk into it. Then he turned to the viewscreen, where the stars were streaming by, and took on a look of contentment.

"I don't think you understand," said Nikolas. "The Ubarrak will destroy us on sight."

"I understand perfectly," said the alien, his mouth spreading again in a smile.

Nikolas thought about trying to incapacitate the bastard, but he knew that he would fail. And then there would be one more pale, shriveled corpse on the *Iktoj'ni*.

No, he thought, *I'll bide my time. Eventually, he'll let his guard down. He has to sleep sometime.*

He had barely completed the thought when the alien sent words into his mind: *I don't, actually. Not anymore.*

"Nonetheless," he added out loud, "assault me if you like. It won't make any difference. We'll still follow the course we're following now."

Nikolas's heart sank in his chest. The alien might not have been as scary as the Ubarrak, with all their ships and their armaments, but he was starting to come in a close second.

Chapter Two

PICARD WAS STUDYING a block of text on his desktop monitor when he heard the sound of chimes, announcing the presence of someone outside his ready room door.

"Come," he said.

The doors opened on command, admitting Picard's friend and first officer, Gilaad Ben Zoma. As usual, Ben Zoma's expression was a cheerful one—until he saw the captain's.

"Must be pretty grim," he observed, "whatever it is."

"I am afraid so," said Picard, leaning back in his chair. With a gesture, he indicated the monitor screen. "These are the charges Admiral McAteer will bring against me. He was nice enough to send them in advance."

Actually, niceness had nothing to do with it. They both knew that it was a requirement of the proceeding.

"What does he say?" asked Ben Zoma, pulling out the chair opposite the captain's.

"Nothing good, I assure you."

Ben Zoma had had the pleasure of listening to McAteer's objections in person, when he and the admiral were working together against the D'prayl. Still, he wanted to hear the specifics.

"For instance?" he said.

Picard sighed. "I never hailed the Nuyyad in accordance with Starfleet protocols, thereby depriving them of the opportunity to tell their side of the story. Instead, I destroyed the vessel pursuing us. Then I attacked another of their vessels—the one in orbit around Magnia. And to add insult to injury, I went after the Nuyyad's supply depot.

"What is worse, according to the admiral, is my reliance on the word of Serenity Santana, whose information had already proven unreliable. In fact, he says, the Federation still has no concrete proof that the Nuyyad represent any threat whatsoever."

Ben Zoma made a sound of disgust. "Starfleet itself was suspicious of the Nuyyad, or it wouldn't have sent us to their galaxy in the first place. And we were attacked almost immediately after we crossed the barrier—a battle in which Captain Ruhalter and several others were killed."

"It's true that I was relying at least partly on the word of Serenity Santana," Picard conceded.

"However," Ben Zoma pointed out, "you received

the same information from a second source—Jomar."

"True," said the captain. Jomar was a Kelvan, and therefore at odds with Santana's people. Yet his description of the Nuyyad as unrelenting aggressors agreed with Santana's.

"And you were hardly in a position to observe protocols," said Ben Zoma. "The *Stargazer* was badly damaged—by the very people McAteer would have had you hail. If you hadn't destroyed them, they would have destroyed *us*."

Picard frowned. "Had the Nuyyad been less hostile to begin with, or had I enjoyed a wider array of options, or had the stakes not been so high . . . of course I might have proceeded differently. But under the circumstances, I do not see that I had a viable alternative."

"Nor do I," said Ben Zoma.

"Thank you," said the captain.

"Don't mention it," said his friend. Unfortunately, Ben Zoma wasn't the one he would have to convince.

"Captain?" came a voice over the intercom. It belonged to Elizabeth Wu, the petite but efficient woman who served as the ship's second officer.

"Have we arrived at Pandril?" Picard asked.

"We have, sir. Lieutenant Asmund is establishing an orbit now."

The captain turned to Ben Zoma. "Care to come along and see Vigo off?"

The first officer quirked a smile. "Of course. There should be someone there he actually *likes*."

*   *   *

Nikolas had spent hours carrying out the chilling task of lugging corpses to the *Iktoj'ni*'s main cargo hold.

The lighter ones he had slung over his shoulder. The heavier ones he had dragged by their ankles. None of them were easy, and they had gotten progressively harder as time went on.

But it didn't seem right to leave his crewmates where they had fallen—especially those stationed on the bridge, whom the alien telekinetically tossed aside whenever he felt they were in his way. So Nikolas had gone through the cargo hauler deck by deck and compartment by compartment, locating the deceased and laying them in rows, side by side.

One of the first bodies he discovered in the engine room was that of Shockey, the redheaded woman who had helped him stop a fight and then tended to the knife wound he had suffered. She had been lying at the foot of a console—more than likely her post in the event of an alert.

Nikolas had liked Shockey. She had been so direct, so down to earth, so clued in to the ways things worked on the *Iktoj'ni*. But then, a lot of his crewmates had been likable—back when they were still alive.

He had collected thirty-three bodies—more than two-thirds of the crew—and was about to pick up his thirty-fourth when he heard a proximity siren go off. It was a security feature the captain had never seen a need for, but Nikolas had set it before he left the bridge. After all, Rejjerin wasn't in charge any longer, and he wanted to know if someone was approaching the ship.

Fortunately, the mineral formations hadn't invaded

the lower decks yet, so Nikolas was able to reach the turbolift at a limping, stiff-legged run. Moments later it deposited him on the bridge level, which had become even thicker with the alien's obstructions and therefore necessitated slower going.

Still, he reached the bridge in a matter of minutes, bursting in to see that the alien was standing beside the captain's chair. He seemed unperturbed by the sound of the alarm, his attention focused on the forward viewscreen.

As far as Nikolas could tell, there was nothing on it but the Doppler rush of stars. But if the alarm had gone off, there had to be something more.

Slipping into the embrace of the navigation station, Nikolas ran a sensor sweep. It showed him that a ship was indeed approaching. He polled the sensors for more information—and got it.

The vessel was Ubarrak—an *Ayatani*-class battle cruiser, as big and powerful as any warship in the sector. And her weapons batteries had been powered up, which meant that her captain was anticipating a fight.

"There's a warship out there," said Nikolas.

"I am aware of it," the alien told him, his composure undisturbed.

"This is just a cargo hauler. We don't stand a chance."

His companion glanced at him, then shrugged his massive shoulders. "We shall see."

He doesn't know what he's up against, Nikolas thought. *And by the time he realizes his mistake, it'll be too late.*

"You can still turn back," he said.

The alien grunted, as if the human had said something funny. But he made no move to turn their ship around.

Nikolas had tried it the easy way. Now he had to try something else. Without warning, he darted across the bridge to get to the helm controls, hoping to bring the ship about.

But as soon as he got near the console, he was greeted with a flash of blue-white energy—one that would have cooked him to a crisp if he had come a little closer.

His nostrils full of ozone, Nikolas glared at the alien. "You don't know what you're doing. All you're going to accomplish is getting us killed."

The alien didn't seem moved in the least. He was still taking in the sight of stars streaming by on the viewscreen, his silver eyes gleaming majestically.

"Do you understand what I'm saying?" Nikolas demanded. "If we go up against that ship, we'll be destroyed."

"Perhaps," said the alien. He turned a sidelong glance on the human, cold enough to turn his insides to ice. "And then again . . . perhaps not."

Picard had been dreaming—something about the marathon on Danula II that he had won as a freshman at the Academy—when he was roused by his second officer's voice on the intercom.

"Sir?" said Wu.

"Picard here," he said, sitting up in bed and running his fingers through his hair.

"Sorry to bother you, sir, but we're being hailed by

an unidentified cargo vessel. Whoever's in command wants to speak with you—and you alone."

"Have they given any indication of what they want?" he asked, pulling aside his covers and swinging his legs out of bed.

"None," came the answer.

"Very well," said the captain. "I will take it here in my quarters."

"Aye, sir."

Padding across the carpeted deck to his closet, Picard took out a clean uniform and slipped it on. Then he sat down in front of the small, space-efficient workstation in the anteroom of his quarters and accepted the communication.

Instantly, the Federation insignia on the screen—a disk displaying a field of gleaming stars resting in the embrace of twin laurel wreaths—gave way to a different image entirely.

It was that of a woman, and a very beautiful woman at that. She had long black hair gathered into a ponytail and eyes the color of rich, dark chocolate. And it wasn't the first time the captain had seen her . . .

Though the last time had been in another galaxy.

Ben Zoma moved his bishop from level 2 to level 3 on the three-dimensional chessboard, then sat back in his chair. "You really think 'brilliant' is the right word, Lieutenant?"

"I do," Urajel confirmed from her seat on the other side of the table as she studied the multilevel chessboard with her shiny black eyes.

She was an Andorian, one of the brighter stars in Mister Simenon's engineering section. And she had a refreshing way of speaking her mind that had always appealed to the first officer, though never more than now.

"I have served with some remarkably resourceful people," Urajel continued, speaking just loudly enough to be heard over the buzz in the observation lounge, "and I can't recall any of them devising such a novel way to communicate."

She was talking about the maneuver Ben Zoma had pulled off just a handful of days earlier. Stuck in an unfamiliar craft that he had borrowed from an armada of hostile aliens, prevented from contacting the *Stargazer*—or any of the other Federation ships lined up against the invaders—by jamming signals, he had nonetheless found a way to defuse the situation.

After all, the aliens didn't really want to fight. They just wanted to retrieve someone who belonged to them, an individual whom the Federation would willingly relinquish once they confirmed his true identity.

But it was Ben Zoma's job to get that information across—at the very least, the part about the possibility of avoiding bloodshed—before the battle got under way.

So he took a roll of flat, pale foodstuff, dyed it with a message Picard alone would understand, and sent it floating out into the void. Seeing the message—a reference to the Picard family vineyard—the captain sent up a red flag. And soon after, what might have been a bloodbath of historical proportions was rendered moot.

It *was* the cleverest thing he had ever done. And

being human, he wanted Urajel to go on complimenting him. But he couldn't be too obvious about it.

"You know," said Ben Zoma, "you're liable to give me a swelled head with that talk."

Urajel made a sound of disdain. "You wouldn't hesitate to remonstrate with someone who had done a poor job, would you? Then why stint on praise?"

"Because it's embarrassing," he explained.

The engineer looked at him with a gleam of skepticism in her eyes. "With all due respect, sir, you don't seem embarrassed in the least. You seem quite pleased."

"Only because I'm trying to accept what you're saying in the spirit in which you've said it."

"I see. So you're merely being open-minded, receptive to the perspectives of another culture."

He nodded. "Exactly."

"Permission to speak freely, sir?"

"You've got it," the first officer told her.

"That might be the most obvious lie I've heard all day."

The first officer watched Urajel's gaze flicker over the game's three boards. "You think so?"

"Yes, sir. And by the way," she said, transporting her queen from the third level to the first, "checkmate."

Ben Zoma stared at Urajel's queen, which along with her rook had placed his king in an untenable position. Somehow, he had overlooked that possibility.

Smiling ruefully, he said, "Next time you say I'm brilliant, it would be nice if you allowed me to believe it for a while."

The Andorian nodded. "I'll try to remember that, sir."

Abruptly, the captain's voice filled the lounge. "Commander Ben Zoma, please join me in my ready room."

"Acknowledged," said the first officer.

Ben Zoma turned to Urajel again and shrugged. "Duty calls. But I'd like a rematch sometime."

"As you wish," the engineer told him.

Then Ben Zoma left the lounge and made his way up to the bridge level. As he exited the turbolift and headed for the captain's sanctum, he exchanged glances with Commander Wu. But she didn't seem to have an inkling as to why he had been summoned.

Pausing outside Picard's door, the first officer waited to be admitted. Then he entered the room and saw his friend sitting behind his desk, a quizzical expression on his face.

"What now?" Ben Zoma asked as the ready room door slid closed behind him.

"You won't believe this," Picard told him, "but I have just spoken with Serenity Santana."

The first officer looked askance at his friend and superior officer. "You're joking, right?"

"Not at all."

Ben Zoma's mind raced from the impossible to the merely improbable. "But that would mean . . ."

"That is correct," Picard confirmed. "She is back on our side of the barrier."

Chapter Three

PICARD REMEMBERED how it had been.

"Soon?" he asked.

"Very," she said.

Then they came over the rise and he found himself looking down on the place she had described. She had come close to doing it justice, but no words could have captured its beauty. As the wind blew roughly through his hair, he said as much.

"You see?" she said, her smile mischievous in the mountain sunshine, her eyes as soft and dark as liquid obsidian. "I don't lie about everything."

He frowned. It seemed so long ago. And yet it had only been a matter of months.

As she pulled his shirt off him, her eyes were drawn to his scar. Her fingers, tiny creatures full of curiosity, explored the shape and dimension of the damaged flesh.

"How?" she asked.

"An indiscretion," he said. "A blade in the wrong hands. And an artificial heart."

"Don't your people have cosmetic surgery?"

"They do," he said. "And maybe someday I'll let them take care of it. But for now, I like the reminder."

She looked up at him slyly. "And your heart? It's an adequate replacement for the one you lost?"

He smiled a little, brushing her cheek with the back of his hand. "There is a way to find out . . ."

For all he knew, he would never get the chance to see her again. This would be it for them.

The lake water was cold on her skin. He could tell by the gooseflesh on her arm as she reached up to him.

"It's not as bad as it looks," she said. "Trust me."

As he lowered himself into its depths, he saw that she was right. The water wasn't as bad as it looked, the bite of cold quickly giving way to an awakening, as if his every pore were independently aware of everything around it.

And of course, of her as well.

She had known the reality of the situation. They were, after all, from different places.

He opened his eyes and saw her lying beside him on the grass, her skin bronze in the flawless sunlight. He didn't want to wake her, didn't want the moment to end.

But she must have heard him stir, because she reached for him and laid her hand on his shoulder. Her touch was warm and delicate, like the feathers of an exotic bird.

Covering her hand with his, he closed his eyes again and dreamed of waking beside her.

It had been like a dream, and dreams were made to end.

One moment, the light in her eyes was alive. The next, a shadow had swallowed it.

Setting his teeth against the inevitable, he looked back over his shoulder and saw that the sun had crossed behind a treetop. The day was growing longer, thinner.

They still had some time together, but not much. Not as much as he would have liked. After all, he had another lover, waiting patiently for him in the star-pricked night that overhung the day.

And her name was Stargazer.

But somehow Serenity was back. She had found him, despite the vast gulf of space that separated them.

The question, Picard thought as he stood on the transporter pad and waited for Ben Zoma, *is why?*

A moment later, the doors to the transporter room opened and the first officer arrived. With a nod to Goetz, the red-haired operator on duty, Ben Zoma mounted the pad and took his place beside the captain.

"Sir," he said.

"Commander," Picard said in return.

Goetz made some last-second adjustments, then looked up from her controls at the captain. "Ready, sir."

"Energize," said Picard.

Suddenly, he and Ben Zoma were somewhere

else—on a much smaller transporter platform in a dim, dingy cargo hold. There were three figures standing in front of them, a male and two females, all of them dressed in snug-fitting, dark green garb—and all of them carrying weapon holsters on their hips.

They looked one hundred percent human. But if they were from Magnia, as Serenity was, it was only their ancestors who had been human. They themselves were something more.

"Captain Picard, Commander Ben Zoma," said one of the women, "please come with me." Her tightly braided hair was a pale, pure yellow, her eyes as green as the sea.

Picard wondered how strong her powers were. Could she move a drinking glass without touching it? Tell him what he was thinking about at that very moment?

No doubt, Ben Zoma was wondering the same thing. But then, he, too, had met the Magnians before.

"Very well," said the captain. Then he allowed the woman to escort him and his first officer out of the hold.

As they passed the other two Magnians, Picard saw how closely the pair studied him. Their curiosity was understandable. He had helped liberate their world from an oppressor—one they hadn't been able to resist, for all their power. Had the captain been one of them, he would have been curious too.

Without another word, the blond woman led the way out of the hold and into a narrow, sporadically lit corridor. Turning left, she followed the bend of the passage for a few moments. Then she stopped in front of a sliding door and placed her hand over a copper-colored plate on the bulkhead.

After a second or two the door hissed open, and the blonde motioned for Picard to enter. Doing so, he found himself in a lounge of sorts, albeit a cheerless one. In the center of the room, there was a round table at which two figures were seated.

One of them was Serenity Santana, looking every bit as darkly beautiful as Picard remembered her. Perhaps even more so, if such a thing was possible.

The other figure was a member of a species Picard had never seen before. He was arrayed in a bronze breastplate and coarse, dark garments—a large, fleshy-looking specimen with tiny black eyes and a fringe of oily-looking hair falling from an otherwise smooth scalp.

The captain felt an immediate aversion to the fellow. It wasn't his looks, though they were certainly repulsive by human standards. It was the way he comported himself—as if he were superior to Picard, Ben Zoma, and even Santana, as if he were in fact doing them a favor just by being there.

"Captain Picard," said Serenity, getting to her feet and speaking with surprising formality—for the benefit of her companion and Ben Zoma, the captain imagined, since he and she would have had no need to do so on their own.

"Miss Santana," Picard responded, in the same vein.

What he would have preferred to do was take her in his arms, and he believed she would have preferred that as well. But this was neither the time nor the place for such intimacies.

Serenity turned to Ben Zoma. "Commander. It's good to see you again."

The first officer smiled. "Same here," he said, though not without a few obvious reservations.

After all, as Admiral McAteer had taken pains to point out, Santana hadn't been entirely honest with them the last time they met. It was only fair to wonder what she was up to.

"Gentlemen," she said, indicating her hulking companion, "I would like you to meet Dojjaron, Sword-Bearer and Foremost Elder . . . of the Nuyyad Alliance."

For a moment, Picard believed he had heard incorrectly. Then he saw the uncharacteristic frown on Santana's face and realized he had heard perfectly after all.

Picard turned to the alien, who lifted his chin as he endured the human's scrutiny. Finally, he turned back to Serenity. "You did say . . . *Nuyyad* Alliance?"

She nodded. "Yes."

"The same Nuyyad Alliance," said Dojjaron, in a voice that was like pieces of metal grinding together, "that you encountered on the other side of the barrier."

Picard didn't understand.

When he last saw Serenity, she was thanking him for his help in freeing her world from Nuyyad domination. Now she seemed to be in league with one of her people's enemies.

Clearly, something had changed.

"Pardon me for being blunt," said Picard, "but I am

surprised. I was led to believe that peaceful relations with the Nuyyad were . . . unlikely at best."

"They were," Serenity conceded.

"And yet," said Dojjaron, "here I sit before you." He made a rasping sound deep in his throat—something that sounded vaguely like laughter, but might well have been something else.

After all, Picard had destroyed some of the Nuyyad's warships, and then torn apart their supply depot for an encore. He doubted that Dojjaron would find that funny.

Then again, the captain knew precious little about the Nuyyad, and there was no accounting for alien tastes. Unlikely as it seemed, his actions may have been a source of amusement to them.

"Obviously," said Serenity, "we didn't dream we would be helping the Nuyyad." She glanced at Dojjaron. "But then, we also didn't expect them to come back so quickly from the damage we had inflicted on them."

Picard frowned. "Did they attack Magnia a second time?"

"No," said Serenity. "They had bigger game to hunt—the one they had already set their sights on."

"The Federation," said Ben Zoma.

"Indeed," said Dojjaron, without a hint of self-consciousness or restraint, though he was addressing citizens of the very union the Nuyyad had targeted. "Had you simply liberated Magnia and stopped there, we would probably have licked our wounds and looked elsewhere for conquest. But the destruction of our depot was an insult, a hand in the face. It gave us even more reason to look in the direction of your homeworlds."

Not exactly the intended result, Picard reflected.

Serenity picked up the story. "Less than four Magnian months after our attack on the depot, the Nuyyad dispatched a scout ship across the galactic barrier. Its job was to map out a route for conquest, which the Nuyyad would pursue when they were ready again to make their push."

"Of course," Dojjaron noted, "we had never crossed the barrier ourselves, but we often traded with those who had. So we knew enough to shield our crew from the radiation that affected Santana's ancestors." He grunted. "Unfortunately, there was an accident in the course of our crossing."

"Not a big one," Serenity observed. "But it left one small portion of their vessel unshielded for a couple of moments—and a couple of moments was all it took."

Picard winced. "Someone was exposed."

"Obviously," said the Nuyyad. "A low-level technician named Brakmaktin. As our ship left the barrier behind, he just seemed weak, stunned. But soon after, he began to change."

Ignoring Dojjaron's remark, Picard listened with growing concern as the alien laid out the details. They sounded all too familiar, given what the captain knew of Gary Mitchell's experience some seventy-five years earlier.

Mitchell had been an officer on the *Enterprise* of that era, a *Constitution*-class vessel that got too close to the galactic barrier. Its energies amplified his existing extrasensory talents, transforming him into a superman who was eventually destroyed by his own captain.

But the *Enterprise* wasn't the first vessel to run afoul of the barrier. Two full centuries before Mitchell's exposure, a Terran ship called the *Valiant* had passed through it on a journey of exploration. One of her crewmen became so powerful that the *Valiant*'s captain blew up his ship rather than allow the fellow to return to Earth.

The survivors of the *Valiant,* who outran her destruction in escape pods, went on to found a civilization of their own—the one from which Serenity and her comrades sprang. They called it Magnia, after a concept put forth by a visionary Terran architect.

Some of those first Magnians had powers of their own, but not of the magnitude exhibited by Mitchell or their fellow crewman, because their extrasensory abilities weren't as strong. The same was true of their descendants.

However, Brakmaktin was like Mitchell, if Dojjaron's account could be believed. His level of power was significant right from the start, manifesting itself in demonstrations of telepathy, telekinesis, and computer-like manipulations of data.

"It didn't take long for Brakmaktin to seize control of the scout ship," Dojjaron continued. "But like any Nuyyad, he couldn't be content with what he had. He attacked another vessel on this side of the barrier and boarded it, leaving the battle-scored scout ship behind."

"Fortunately," said Serenity, "there was a survivor on the scout ship, a female who managed to restore the vessel's shields and take it back through the barrier."

"Whereupon she warned us that an *aberration* was on the loose—just before she perished from her injuries." Dojjaron nodded approvingly. "She was a warrior."

"An aberration," echoed Ben Zoma. "Interesting way to put it."

"You have to understand," said Serenity, "the Nuyyad are instinctively repelled by physical anomalies, especially those that grant an individual an advantage over the rest of the pack. So the notion of a Nuyyad superbeing running around on the loose was intolerable to them, even if he was all the way on the other side of the barrier."

"Brakmaktin is by his nature an affront," the Nuyyad declared, his wide, peg-toothed mouth twisting savagely, "as well as a challenge. And a threat."

"I see," said Picard.

"Normally," Dojjaron went on, "we would have hunted him down on our own, as is our custom. But according to the reports we have received from our trading partners, your space is filled with a number of political entities, any one of which might have blundered across us and rendered our mission impossible to carry out."

"Blundered," said Ben Zoma, smiling tautly. "You do have a way with words, Foremost Elder."

Picard put a hand on his friend's forearm and said, "Please go on."

It was Serenity who took up the thread. "Under the circumstances, the Nuyyad were most familiar with your Federation. But given the nature of your previous contact, they didn't think you would greet them with open arms."

"We needed a go-between," Dojjaron expanded, "someone your *Federation* would be more inclined to trust." His spin on the word made clear his disdain.

Refusing to rise to the bait, the captain glanced at Serenity. "Someone like the Magnians, I gather."

Dojjaron nodded his massive head. "And *her* in particular. As you know, she was one of the first two Magnians to make contact with your people. It made sense for her to accompany me here and seek out your *Stargazer.*"

"Because," said Picard, "I was the only Starfleet captain who really knew her, and would consider helping her."

"Of course," said Dojjaron.

"Naturally," said Serenity, "we were distrustful of the Nuyyad. They had seized our world, subjected us to their tyranny—and forced us to draw a Federation vessel across the barrier so they could get a look at her."

Dojjaron didn't object to her choice of words. Rather, he seemed to take pride in them.

"However," Serenity continued, "we couldn't see what the Nuyyad had to gain by lying to us. Passage through the barrier? They had already accomplished that without help from Magnia. Contact with the Federation? Maybe—but for what purpose?"

Off the top of his head, the captain couldn't come up with a motive either.

"On the contrary," said Serenity, "if they were planning on conquering the Federation, they would have hurt their chances by alerting us to the fact."

True, thought Picard. After all, he and his crew had risked their lives to help the Magnians; Serenity's people had every reason to want to return the favor.

"In the end," she said, "it came down to one thing: if there was even a chance that the Nuyyad were telling the truth, and a superbeing had been unleashed on your galaxy, how could we look the other way—especially when he would eventually become a threat to our galaxy as well?"

"So you allowed Dojjaron to accompany you across the barrier," the captain said.

Serenity nodded. "As an expert on Nuyyad physiology and behavior. But we insisted that he come alone, to make sure there wasn't any funny business."

Funny business, Picard thought. It was an odd phrase, one that hadn't been widely used for hundreds of years. But as he had been reminded before, Magnian culture had developed differently from the one the *Valiant* left on Earth.

"An expert," he said, bringing his thoughts back on track.

"Yes," said Serenity. "That and nothing more."

"I see," said Picard.

Despite his feelings for Serenity, he wasn't ready to jump at her request. However, he had heard enough from her and Dojjaron to want to know more. "How did you find me?"

Serenity's mouth hinted at a smile. "Last time I was

on the *Stargazer,* I took the liberty of examining some of her flight logs. That gave me an idea of her customary patrol routes."

The captain felt a spurt of resentment. "It is good to know how far I can trust you."

Serenity shrugged. "I confessed, didn't I?"

"You did," Picard conceded. "And I wonder . . . what impropriety will you be confessing next time we meet?"

Serenity didn't go through the motion of giving him an answer. It seemed clear that she still had her own agenda, even if it often appeared to dovetail with the captain's.

There was something else. "Our scans," he observed, "indicate a number of other Magnians on your vessel. Who are they?"

She mentioned a few names that he recognized, including that of Guard Daniels, the Magnian who had accompanied her the first time she left her galaxy to enter Federation space. "You wouldn't know any of the others."

"Why so many?" Picard asked.

"It's a task force," she explained. "We put it together for the purpose of confronting Brakmaktin and neutralizing him. All we need from you is help in finding him."

"If this individual is as powerful as you claim," Picard asked, "why limit yourself to a task force? Why not use the full range of resources at your disposal, including those available on the *Stargazer?"*

"Because," said Serenity, firmly but without scorn,

"you and your people would only get in the way."

Picard looked at her. "Really."

"We're Magnians," she said. "You know some of the things of which we're capable, especially when we act in concert. Even if we hadn't had an inkling of your location, we could have tracked you down with the power of our minds."

"Then why not locate Brakmaktin yourselves?" asked Ben Zoma.

"Nuyyad brains work differently," said Serenity. "Their thoughts are difficult for us to pick up."

"Of course they are," said Dojjaron.

Serenity went on without breaking stride, having obviously grown accustomed to the Nuyyad's attitude. "That's why we need your help, Captain. You know this part of space as well as anyone. And Brakmaktin is certain to leave some kind of trail."

Picard frowned. The Magnians were powerful beings—he couldn't dispute that. But the thought of serving as a bird dog didn't sit well with him.

"In any case," said Dojjaron, "we cannot sit here picking our back teeth. Time is our enemy."

"Yes," said Serenity. "The longer Brakmaktin's power has to develop, the more dangerous he'll become—and the more likely it is he'll find his way to a populated planet."

The captain didn't need her to paint a picture. He had never encountered a superbeing, but he could imagine the kind of havoc such an individual could wreak.

"Assuming for the moment that this Brakmaktin fellow actually exists," he said, "what is he likely to do when he comes in contact with such a population? Enslave them?"

It was a valid question. After all, Gary Mitchell—prior to his untimely demise—had begun thinking of himself as a god, and gods required worshippers.

"It is more complicated than that," said Dojjaron. "My people are the product of a harsh, largely barren world, where food and shelter are in short supply. Those who do not compete effectively for these resources find their bones bleaching in the sun."

"You're fighters," Ben Zoma observed.

"Fighters, yes," said the foremost elder. "Stubborn ones. But we are also highly procreative in comparison to other species, giving birth to large numbers of offspring as frequently as every sixty-eight solar days."

"And their days are shorter than those on Magnia," Serenity contributed. "Or, for that matter, those on Earth. On the average, a Nuyyad female of prime childbearing age produces twenty-four live offspring in a Federation standard year."

Picard glanced at his first officer, who was equally impressed. It was easy to see why the Nuyyad had become conquerors—initially on their own world, and later on more fertile ones. They were driven by an intense biological imperative that required them to find more and more space for their progeny.

"Like any Nuyyad warrior," said Dojjaron, "Brakmaktin's primary concern will be to create a safe environment for the offspring of his clan."

"But his clan is back on the other side of the barrier," the captain pointed out. "And there are no Nuyyad females at hand to start a new one."

"He will not need females," Dojjaron told him. "In their absence, Nuyyad males can produce offspring on their own."

"You mean they can clone themselves?" the captain asked.

"In essence," said Dojjaron, "yes."

Asexual reproduction was a fairly common ability among simple animals. However, it was a most uncommon one among the galaxy's more complex species.

Nor was it good news. The effects of the barrier on an exposed individual could be passed on from generation to generation, as the Magnians had amply demonstrated.

However, none of Magnia's founders had been transformed as radically as Gary Mitchell, so their powers had been more modest. And the presence of *un*transformed individuals had gradually watered down the gene pool.

But there wouldn't be any untransformed females to water down Brakmaktin's genes. His progeny could all grow up to become as obscenely powerful as their parent.

"And you think that is what Brakmaktin will do?" Picard asked. "Create offspring?"

"Without question," said Dojjaron. "Given the magnitude of his power and his isolation from other Nuyyad, the impulse to multiply will be irresistible. It will take place quickly and it will take place often."

It was a grim thought.

"Twenty-four the first year," Ben Zoma thought out loud. "And twenty-four more the second, and the third . . ."

"And every year thereafter," said Serenity, "for as long as Brakmaktin is capable of bearing them."

Dojjaron made a face. "And eventually, his offspring will begin to bear offspring of their own."

The captain tried to imagine a galaxy full of superpowerful Nuyyad. It wouldn't possess the slightest resemblance to the one he knew.

"How can we stop him?" he asked.

"There is a way," Dojjaron said. "After Brakmaktin creates a suitable environment for his young, and his body begins to change so he can reproduce, he will enter a period of dormancy. Like any Nuyyad, he will be vulnerable at this time."

"That," said Serenity, "is when we must strike."

"Assuming we've gotten within striking distance," Ben Zoma noted.

She nodded.

Picard saw now why the Magnians hadn't gone directly to the Federation. The last time Serenity crossed the barrier, she and Guard Daniels had been detained for weeks while Starfleet Command decided what to do with them.

And this time she had a Nuyyad foremost elder at her side. It might have been months before Picard's superiors reached any kind of decision regarding them. If Brakmaktin was half as dangerous as Serenity and

Dojjaron contended, they needed to move a bit more quickly than that.

"You see what we're up against?" she asked.

Picard nodded. "I do."

"Then you'll help?"

The captain considered what he had heard. He couldn't implicitly trust Serenity—not after she had deceived him the last time they met. And he felt compelled to trust Dojjaron even less.

But would she have brought along a Nuyyad—and risked the immense red flag raised by his presence—if she had intended to deceive the captain a second time? Would it not have been a lot easier to accomplish that quietly, on her own?

Or had Serenity brought Dojjaron precisely *because* his presence made treachery seem so unlikely? Was she just using the Nuyyad as a stalking horse?

And if she was, what kind of scheme did she have in mind this time? How would it benefit Magnia? And would it, at the same time, hurt someone else?

So many possibilities. And each one came with its own colorful collection of pitfalls.

Serenity's dark eyes caught the light. "You don't trust me," she observed.

Picard frowned. It wasn't easy to deal with someone who could read minds. "Not completely, no."

"With all due respect," she said, "I don't see this as a difficult decision. We should encounter some evidence of Brakmaktin's power before too long. If we do, we keep going. And if we don't, you can turn your ship around."

It made sense. But the captain still wasn't going to rush his decision. It was too serious a matter for him not to get it right.

"I will contact you," he told Serenity, "as soon as I have had a chance to digest all you have said."

Dojjaron looked disbelieving, as if Picard were the biggest idiot he had ever encountered.

Serenity, on the other hand, was more measured in her response. "I beg you," she said, "digest it carefully. It may be the most important decision you've ever made."

With that ominous advice ringing in his ears, Picard got up and allowed himself to be escorted back to the transporter room.

Chapter Four

PICARD SAT BACK in his plastiform chair and regarded Ben Zoma, who was seated on the other side of his desk. "Well?" he asked. "What do you think?"

"I think," said the first officer, "that the foremost elder could use a lesson in manners."

Picard frowned. "You know what I mean."

Ben Zoma shrugged. "It sounds like Santana's telling the truth. But then, I thought that the first time we met her."

"Wherein lies the problem," said the captain. "Do we refuse her request for assistance, and risk allowing a potentially hostile superbeing to roam free? Or do we give her what she wants and take a chance on being duped?"

"Again," Ben Zoma noted.

"Yes," said Picard, tasting ashes. "Again."

For a while, neither of them spoke. They were too busy thinking, too busy weighing options.

"It's times like these," Ben Zoma said at last, "that I'm glad they made *you* captain and not *me*."

"Thank you," said Picard. "I knew I could count on my first officer for wisdom and insight."

"What do you want me to say?" asked Ben Zoma. "That there's a way to be certain of Santana's intentions? There isn't. We both know that." He tilted his head to one side, as if it gave him a better perspective on the captain. "And we also know you've already made up your mind to help them."

Picard began to protest—until he realized that his friend was right. "I have, haven't I?" He just couldn't ignore the sort of threat Serenity had described.

He was, after all, an officer in Starfleet, charged with protecting life both within the Federation and without. If there was any possibility at all that Serenity was telling the truth, it fell to him to investigate it.

All the while, of course, holding on to a healthy amount of skepticism.

"So once more into the breach," said Ben Zoma, "with your friend Santana for company."

Picard nodded. "It certainly looks that way."

"Of course," said the first officer, "if it turns out that she's lying again, we'll just be giving McAteer more ammunition for his competency hearing."

Picard dismissed the notion with a wave of his hand. "If Serenity is deceiving us again and we have fallen for it, I will save the admiral the trouble."

"You mean . . . you'll resign?"

The captain nodded, meaning every word of it. "In a heartbeat."

Nikolas watched the Ubarrak cruiser on the bridge's viewscreen loom larger and larger, a shadow of death slowly blotting out the spray of stars.

He had studied Ubarrak spacecraft thoroughly enough at the Academy to identify their weaknesses, of which there were several. If he were on a Federation starship, he would have known how to take advantage of them.

But Nikolas wasn't that fortunate. He was on an Yridian cargo hauler, and an old one at that, with tactical systems that had been outdated and inadequate even before the alien with the silver eyes saw fit to destroy them.

Now, the *Iktoj'ni* had no shield emitters, no weapons batteries, no conceivable way to defend herself. The cruiser's weapons officer had to be thinking it was his birthday, or whatever occasion his people liked to celebrate.

Yet Nikolas's companion remained unfazed in his growing maze of mineral deposits. He regarded the warship as if she were a novelty, an amusement—as if the idea of the *Iktoj'ni* being reduced to atoms, and her two living occupants along with her, was of no particular relevance to him.

The human would have tried again to get them out of there, but it was no use. The alien clearly wasn't going to allow that. For some unfathomable reason, he wanted to confront the Ubarrak.

"What in blazes do you think you're going to accomplish?" Nikolas asked him.

The alien didn't bother answering. He just kept staring at the viewscreen.

A moment later, the Ubarrak's weapons ports began to glow with a sickly bluish light. *We're in weapons range,* Nikolas thought. *Any moment now, they'll let us have it.*

The alien had to be thinking the same thing. However, the knowledge obviously wasn't moving him. *Was he insane?* the human wondered. *Was that why he faced death so carelessly?*

Suddenly, the warship began belching packets of deadly azure energy, one after another. They were photon projectiles. Nikolas had seen pictures of them back at the Academy.

In a matter of seconds, they would plow into the cargo hauler like daggers and rip her apart. The human watched them with morbid fascination, bracing himself for the impact.

But it never came. The packets of blue brilliance splashed against the viewscreen, threatening all kinds of violence, but somehow they failed to make their presence felt.

Nikolas didn't get it. Giddily, he checked the monitors on the helm console. None of them registered any damage to the transport. Not even a scratch.

How is that possible? he asked himself.

He looked to his grotesque companion for an explanation—just in time to see the alien turn away from the viewscreen. He actually looked as if he were *bored.*

50

Nikolas returned his attention to the screen, still unable to believe that the Ubarrak's barrage could be so ineffectual. But by then, it had stopped. The warship wasn't firing anymore.

"What happened?" Nikolas muttered, never meaning for anyone to hear the question.

"It's difficult to fire," the alien said in the most casual of tones, "when your mind has been erased."

Erased? The word echoed eerily in Nikolas's mind. An Ubarrak battle cruiser had a complement of nearly a hundred warriors, each one carefully selected and highly trained . . .

But not *this* battle cruiser, he realized with a tightening of his throat. Not anymore.

"Fortunately," the alien added in the same inappropriately casual tone, "their *ship* is in perfect condition."

Picard regarded Serenity Santana's image on his desktop monitor screen. "All right," he said, "I will take you at your word—unless and until you give me reason to do otherwise."

She looked pleased and disappointed at the same time. "Honestly, Jean-Luc, I thought we had learned enough about each other to get past all that."

In fact, the captain had gotten to know Serenity quite well in the couple of days before the *Stargazer* left her galaxy, when he and his crew were restoring the ship to the condition in which she had originally crossed the barrier.

But he knew that she would put Magnia's welfare

ahead of anything else. That made her someone to be treated warily, despite what had transpired between them.

"I wish I could say so," Picard replied.

If Serenity took offense at the remark, it wasn't readily apparent. "You'll get your wish," she said. "Believe me."

They spent the next several minutes discussing the details of the Magnians' transfer to the *Stargazer*. And of course, Dojjaron's. Then they signed off.

It was strange putting aside their passion for each other this way. Nonetheless, it had to be done.

Leaning back in his chair, the captain considered another detail of the mission he had just undertaken. Unfortunately, this one was a little stickier.

His duty, at that juncture, was to get in touch with Starfleet Command and apprise Admiral McAteer of his intention to track down Brakmaktin. However, he knew that the admiral would never authorize Picard's involvement in the matter.

Even if McAteer put any faith in Serenity's story, which seemed highly unlikely, he would place the assignment in the hands of a more experienced captain. Greenbriar, for instance. Or Vayishra. Or Van Loon.

But Picard was the one who had crossed the barrier and seen Magnia. He alone, of all the captains in the fleet, knew what Serenity's people were capable of. And he alone had a feel for how far they could be trusted.

Clearly, he was the captain best qualified for this

undertaking. It was his duty to take the initiative—and assume the accompanying risk to his career.

After all, what did he have to lose? Thanks to Mc-Ateer, he was already on the verge of forfeiting his command.

Of course, he would still transmit a message outlining the situation. If Brakmaktin was indeed the threat Dojjaron made him out to be and Picard failed to defuse him, the rest of the fleet would need to know what had happened.

However, it would be strictly a one-way communication.

Nikolas searched the *Iktoj'ni* slowly and painstakingly, wandering through corridor after long, dimly lit corridor, but he couldn't find his friend Locklear. He came across the corpses of a great many other crewmen—all of them stiff and dead, their bodies contorted and their faces drained of blood.

But not Locklear.

Seeing that his friend wasn't in the corridors, Nikolas looked in the cargo hauler's service shafts and cargo bays. But he couldn't find Locklear there either. It was as if he had left the ship, impossible as that seemed.

Still, Nikolas *had* to find his friend. He couldn't just let him lie somewhere, twisted and pale and forgotten. He had to find him and say good-bye to him.

There were fifty sleeping compartments on the cargo hauler, though he couldn't imagine how anyone could have slept through an attack. But one by one,

Nikolas went through those as well. He discovered a few more crewmen and a small horned quadruped that wasn't supposed to be on board. But it was as dead as everyone else, so the breach hardly seemed to matter anymore.

He sat down with the animal and stroked its soft, furry back. It felt stiff and cold underneath its fur.

Suddenly, Nikolas realized that he wasn't on the *Iktoj'ni* anymore. Somehow he was back on the *Stargazer* instead, wearing his cranberry-and-black Starfleet uniform, and the animal he had found was nowhere to be seen.

Allowing that he might have been confused, and that Locklear might have been on the *Stargazer* instead, Nikolas began his search anew. But he still couldn't find his friend, no matter how hard he looked or how many places he checked.

Locklear wasn't in the mess hall or the gymnasium. In sickbay, Nikolas found Greyhorse sitting in his office, but the doctor said that no one had brought Locklear in. Captain Picard and some of his officers were on the bridge, but none of them appeared to have even heard of Locklear.

Finally, as Nikolas was about to admit defeat, a sixth sense told him to look back over his shoulder—and to his relief, there was his pal Locklear. Miraculously, he wasn't even dead. He was standing there grinning as if it were all a big game—the attack on the ship, the alien, even the bodies of their fellow crewmen.

"Why are you smiling?" asked Nikolas.

"I'm not smiling," said his friend. "How can I smile? I'm dead." And right before Nikolas's eyes, the color drained from Locklear's face until he was as pallid as all the other victims of the attack.

Nikolas shook his head and took a step back. "No . . ."

Then Locklear crumpled and hit the deck. But his body didn't make a sound. It was as if he lacked substance, as if he weighed no more than the air around them.

Nikolas knelt beside his friend and saw that his eyeholes were empty. *No,* he thought, correcting himself—Locklear's eyes were still there, lurking in the darkness of their sockets. They had just shriveled like raisins.

"Andreas?" said a voice.

It was different from Locklear's—soft and strong at the same time, and ever so feminine. And the woman to whom it belonged was somewhere nearby.

Nikolas looked up and saw her standing by herself at the far end of the corridor. She had yellow hair twisted into a single braid and startling blue eyes, and a face that made his heart pound in his chest.

Gerda Idun . . . ? he thought.

"Is that you?" he asked, his voice echoing.

"It's me," she said, taking a step toward him, and then another. "I know how bad you feel about your friend, and I want to make your pain go away."

He *did* have pain, almost too much to bear. And if anyone could assuage it, was Gerda Idun.

But she had gone back to the universe she came

from. He had watched her fade away on the transporter platform, enveloped by a column of light.

"How—?" he asked.

She didn't answer. She just came forward to embrace him. But the closer she got, the more her expression began to change.

Nikolas started to fear that Gerda Idun would die too, just like Locklear and Redonna and all the others. He didn't think he could stand it if that happened.

However, she remained solid and vital, her cheeks flushed with life. *She's not dying,* he realized with a pang of relief. But she looked as if she was in some kind of pain, and it seemed to get worse with every step.

"No," he breathed, and got up to help her, though he didn't know what to do. If he couldn't help Locklear or the others, what could he do for Gerda Idun?

But as he came for her, she recoiled and put her hands up. It was as if she didn't want him near her.

"It's all right," he told her. "I don't care what happens to me. I just want to hold you again."

Still, she shrank from him. It was then that he realized it wasn't Gerda Idun who was changing. It was *him.*

His hands were becoming pale and clawlike, and his legs were growing weak—too weak to hold his weight. The life was going out of them. As he sank to his knees, he saw the look on Gerda Idun's face—one of horror and disgust—and that was worse than anything else that could happen to him.

"Please," he said, though his throat was suddenly too dry to utter anything else. "Please . . ."

But the corridor was growing dimmer. It was getting harder and harder to see Gerda Idun. And he was too weak to hold himself up any longer. As he fell forward, helpless to stop himself, he knew with a certainty he had never felt before that he would be dead well before he hit the deck. . . .

Suddenly, there was light all around him—light that was too bright for his eyes. And to Nikolas's surprise, he didn't feel weak anymore. Propping himself up on an elbow, he shaded his eyes and blinked until he could get some idea of where the light was coming from.

It took a while, but he got his answer. It was coming from *everywhere*—the walls as well as the ceiling. But on the *Stargazer,* the only lighting strips were overhead.

Which meant that he wasn't *on* the *Stargazer.* He was somewhere else, he told himself, as the cold sweat of his nightmare began drying on his skin.

And it wasn't the cargo hauler. That much was becoming clear to him, because he didn't feel as if he were in a cavern. But it wasn't until he got to his feet and looked around that it struck him where he might be.

On the Ubarrak ship.

Nikolas could tell by the pictograms cut into the walls. Now that he could see them, there was no mistaking them. They looked exactly like the designs he had studied back at the Academy.

He didn't know how he had gotten there. But clearly, the alien had had something to do with it.

Getting to his feet, Nikolas looked down the corridor in both directions. They looked equally promising to him — which was to say not very. In the end, he picked one direction at random and followed it, his footsteps echoing wildly, until he found something resembling a turbolift.

Getting inside, he took it to its highest level, which was where he knew he would find the ship's bridge. When the doors opened, he found himself at the end of a short hallway with heavily incised bulkheads. There was but one door at the other end.

The last time Nikolas had come out onto a bridge, it was full of corpses slumped over their consoles. He prepared himself for something like that here . . .

And was faced with much the same kind of tableau. There were nearly a dozen thick-necked, uniformed Ubarrak scattered about the command center, some still seated behind their control consoles, others sprawled on the stalagmite-peppered deck—and all of them silent as a tomb.

He moved to get a closer look at one of them, a female who was slumped over a control panel, her face caught in the strobe effect of a dozen blinking lights. Her gaze was vacant, her slitted yellow eyes unfocused in their oversized sockets, lending support to the human's supposition that she was dead.

But a thread of spittle was still descending from the corner of her mouth. And when Nikolas felt her neck, he discerned a pulse under his fingertips. *Damn,* he thought, *she's alive.*

He tried the Ubarrak at the next console—a male this time—and got the same result. What seemed like a corpse at first glance was a still-living being, albeit without awareness of what was going on around him.

Then he remembered what the alien had said, though it seemed like a very long time ago: *"It's difficult to fire when your mind has been erased."*

And Nikolas hadn't been misled. The Ubarrak all looked brain-dead, their bodies still functioning at some basic level though their minds had been destroyed.

Somehow, Nikolas found that even more horrifying than the slaughter of his friends aboard the cargo hauler. It was one thing to die and be removed forever from torment and indignity, and another to remain among the living as mute testimony to an enemy's power.

Easing the male to the deck, Nikolas took his place behind the control panel. It had but one oval-shaped monitor displaying a chart that might have been a fuel consumption trend. It was difficult to say.

Fortunately, Nikolas knew a little Ubarrak. It took him a while, but he was eventually able to punch in the right command to bring up a graphic of the vessel's course.

It appeared as a bright red line on a green and black grid, with the star systems along its path represented as yellow circles. Though it took some doing, Nikolas managed to divine the line's direction—and therefore the battle cruiser's.

The alien was taking them deeper into Ubarrak territory, pursuing the objective he had laid out for himself earlier—the planet whose identity he had plucked out of Nikolas's head.

With his adversary somewhere else, the human took the opportunity to try to bring the vessel about. But the helm wouldn't respond. Apparently, he had been locked out of the controls.

Bastard, he thought.

Next, he accessed the operations function and looked for a way to disable the cruiser's engines. But the alien had placed roadblocks in those command paths as well.

Nikolas's stomach clenched. He hadn't willingly done anything to help the monster, and yet it was his fault that the warship's crew had been turned into vegetables—and his fault as well that the alien was about to descend on an innocent and unsuspecting planetary population.

Unless, of course, Nikolas found a way to stop him.

Chapter Five

LIEUTENANT NOL KASTIIGAN, the purple-jowled Kandilkari chief of the *Stargazer*'s science section, was hardly the most accomplished navigator on the ship. That designation belonged to Gerda Asmund, hands down.

However, Kastiigan *was* a connoisseur of even the most esoteric sensor data, an expertise that enabled him to make more of that information than most other people. It was with this talent in mind that the captain had asked him to lend Gerda a hand.

They knew from the Nuyyad scout's sensor log that she had attacked another vessel and that Brakmaktin had left her at that point. But they didn't know where he had gone. And before they could figure it out, they had to determine the coordinates at which contact with the second vessel had taken place.

The scout's stellar positioning data should have made the task a relatively simple one. However, the pertinent files were far from perfectly preserved. The scout had sustained quite a bit of damage in her battle with the second ship, and the positioning data was only one of the casualties.

Fortunately, the scout had recorded other kinds of information as well—data on plasma waves, neutrino activity, gravimetric imbalances, and so on—all of it gathered through the vessel's long-range sensors. Stored in a different set of logs, it had come through the battle almost completely unscathed.

If Kastiigan could identify a part of space that exhibited the same long-range readings as those picked up by the Nuyyad scout, he might be able to point Gerda in the right direction. At the very least, the captain had believed it was worth a try.

"Anything yet?" asked Daniels, a Magnian with a red mustache who appeared to be Serenity Santana's second-in-command. He had been hovering over Kastiigan for the last half hour or so, ever since he had entered the science section with his security escort.

The science officer turned from his instruments and smiled at the fellow. "Nothing yet. But I assure you, if I do discover something promising, I will let you know."

Daniels nodded. Then he left Kastiigan and joined Bender, one of the other science officers, at her console. Bender had been through some difficult times recently. However, she seemed enthralled by Daniels's presence.

And she wasn't the only member of the crew fascinated by the Magnians. Kastiigan had seen a number of his colleagues exhibiting the same reaction, stealing wide-eyed glances when they thought their visitors weren't looking.

It was understandable. These were people endowed with abilities about which other sentients could only dream. The power to manipulate matter with their minds, for instance. Or to resist energy blasts that would kill lesser beings. Or to absorb information at what seemed like an impossible rate.

Kastiigan was intrigued by the Magnians as well, but not because of their superhuman powers. He was captivated by the fact that they would soon be laying their lives on the line against a threat almost too powerful to imagine.

There was a chance that they would die fighting. A *good* chance, no matter how heroically they acquitted themselves, no matter how ferociously they struggled. And if Brakmaktin prevailed, their sacrifice would eventually be forgotten.

But if Brakmaktin fell somehow, thanks to the Magnians' efforts or otherwise, they would be revered for what they had done. Their story would be told to children by starlight, and its details coveted like precious stones.

They would enjoy a life in death much greater than anything they had before, a life reserved for those who had paid the ultimate price. And because of that, they would never die.

How Kastiigan envied them.

*   *   *

Pug Joseph, acting head of security on the *Stargazer*, was concentrating so hard on reviewing the list of security personnel he had assigned to the Magnians that he almost collided with a Magnian there in the corridor.

As luck would have it, it was the only one he really knew—Serenity Santana, the woman who had dragged Joseph and his crewmates into the thick of her people's battle with the Nuyyad.

Lieutenant Pierzynski was right there with her—a good thing, since the captain had said he wanted their guests accompanied by security officers at all times. It was an order the Magnians hadn't questioned.

"Mister Joseph," Santana said as she got closer, an unmistakable note of pleasure in her voice. "How are you?"

Damn, but she was beautiful. The security chief had managed to forget *how* beautiful.

"Fine," he said. "And you?"

A shadow crossed her face. "A little tired. But then, we've been moving rather quickly."

"To stop this Nuyyad," he said.

"Yes," said Santana. Suddenly, she seemed to shrug off her mantle of care. "I understand you've been promoted."

"Not exactly," said Joseph, with a glance at Pierzynski. "I'm just the *acting* head of security."

Santana shrugged. "I'd be willing to bet that's only a temporary situation."

He looked at her askance. Did she know something

he didn't? She was a telepath, after all. She might have dipped into the captain's mind and read his intentions.

Just as she might have been reading *his* at that very moment. The realization made him blush.

"It was just a figure of speech," Santana told him. "Sorry if I got your hopes up."

"It's all right," he assured her.

But it wasn't, not completely, and he knew that she could tell. She had those powers, after all.

"Well," Santana said, "it's good to see you. I'm sure we'll run into each other again."

"No doubt," said Joseph.

He nodded to Pierzynski. Then he continued down the corridor, doing his best not to think anything at all.

Simenon hefted the phaser rifle—a design that was decidedly different from any he had seen before, with its shorter, thicker barrel, its single handle, and its blue-black casing—and then handed it back to the Magnian. In the soft lighting of the engineering section, the weapon glistened like the hide of some dark, lean-muscled predator.

"It feels lighter than ours," the Gnalish observed.

Vigil O'Shaugnessy nodded, loosening a lock of her sleek brown hair. "That's because it doesn't have a trigger, a keypad for making adjustments in beam width and intensity, or a subspace transceiver assembly."

Simenon looked at her. The subspace transceiver built into every handheld phaser on the *Stargazer* facilitated communication with the ship's computer, preventing phased emissions more powerful than "heavy stun."

In other words, O'Shaugnessy could blow a hole through the *Stargazer*'s hull if she wished. It made Simenon squeamish just thinking about it.

"And you know about our phaser rifles . . . ?" he asked.

O'Shaugnessy smiled. "It wasn't by studying the blueprints, I can tell you that."

Simenon tilted his scaly head to the side. "All our ordnance is—"

"Stowed in the armory," said the Magnian, "behind six inches of duranium-tritanium alloy. I know."

The engineer hated it when someone finished his sentences for him, but he put his pique aside in the interest of cooperation. After all, O'Shaugnessy and her team did represent their ace in the hole.

"I thought your people couldn't perceive anything through walls that thick," he said.

"Most of us can't," O'Shaugnessy confirmed. "However, this is a hand-picked team. We can do things others can't."

Simenon supposed he should be grateful for that. But somehow, he found it disturbing.

Of course, he was no stranger to the Magnians. He had worked with them on the defense of their world, taking their talents into consideration as he amplified the effectiveness of their tactical systems.

The level of esper ability he had encountered was impressive to someone who couldn't overhear a thought or move a teacup with the power of his mind.

But O'Shaugnessy, and those with her, seemed to be capable of even more of that.

How much more? the engineer wondered. And would it be enough to do what they came for?

Ensign Cole Paris was about to touch the pressure-sensitive pad beside the entrance to Jiterica's quarters when he heard voices within.

Clearly, one of them was Jiterica's. The new containment suit Chief Simenon had designed for her made her voice sound more natural than before, but it still wasn't produced by vocal cords.

By contrast, the other voice sounded human. And masculine. Definitely not Commander Wu—who, to Paris's knowledge, was the only member of the crew who had ever visited Jiterica in her quarters.

Besides Paris himself, of course.

In fact, he had come to see Jiterica many times—first as a friend, and in time as a lover. But he had never had to worry about interrupting a visit from someone else.

Paris hesitated, his hand poised by the pad. To that point, he had kept his relationship with Jiterica a secret, reluctant to attract the curiosity of his fellow crewmen.

After all, Jiterica was a low-density being, very different from Paris or anyone else on board. It was only her containment suit, with its built-in force field, that allowed her to maintain a humanoid form. Without it, she would eventually lose control and revert to her natural, gaslike state.

It wasn't that Paris was ashamed of his feelings for Jiterica. He just didn't want people talking about the two of them. What they had together was their business, and no one else's.

At least, that was his take on it. He hadn't asked Jiterica what she thought, but he had a feeling she felt the same way.

Which was why he hesitated to press the pad and announce his presence. If Jiterica was talking to someone, she might not want her guest taking note of Paris's visit.

Then he heard the voices grow louder, and after that there was laughter. It gave rise to something in Paris that he couldn't remember feeling before.

It wasn't a good feeling, either. It was awkward and uncomfortable and insistent, and it made the blood rise to his face.

Damn, he thought, *I'm jealous, aren't I?*

It was absurd. If Jiterica was laughing with somebody, that was a good thing. It meant that she was enjoying herself.

But there was something about that other voice that he didn't like—something untrustworthy, it seemed to him. Maybe it was just his imagination. But Jiterica was so naive, so easy to take advantage of . . .

So easy to hurt.

You're crazy, he told himself. *No one on board would hurt Jiterica. There's nothing to worry about.*

Then he heard that other voice again, and it changed his mind. Setting his jaw, he pressed his hand against the pad and waited for Jiterica to respond.

It took what seemed like a long time before the door finally whispered aside. When it did, Paris saw Jiterica standing in the center of the room.

But she didn't have her containment suit on. She was . . . naked, in all her glittering-ion glory. And she wasn't alone.

"Cole," said Jiterica, "come in."

She gestured to indicate the one who was with her—a man half a head taller than Paris, with short blond hair and a dashing slash of a goatee.

He wasn't a crewman. He was a Magnian. And his smile matched his voice—oily somehow.

"This is Stave," said Jiterica.

Paris felt a rush of blood to his face. He didn't know anything about the man, but he instinctively didn't like him. And he liked even less the fact that Jiterica was standing there in front of him without anything on.

Back on her homeworld, no one wore clothes. Why would they? They were essentially clouds of ions, drifting through the atmosphere on savage chemical winds.

But Jiterica wasn't a cloud at the moment. She had the shape of a humanoid, enforced even without her suit. And there was something indecent about the way Stave was leering at her.

"You ought to put your suit back on," Paris said. And then, realizing how awkward it sounded, he added, "So you won't strain yourself."

Stave chuckled. That sounded oily too. "I was just showing Jiterica what it would be like to walk around without the suit—or the strain."

Only then did Paris understand. Stave was keeping Jiterica's molecules in line with the power of his mind.

Paris had known that the Magnians had superhuman powers, but this was the first time he had seen them in action. It would have been impressive if it didn't feel so . . . improper.

And Jiterica didn't have any sense of what was going on. She didn't *understand*.

"Isn't it wonderful?" she asked Paris.

Stave's smile widened. "I'm glad you like it."

Paris didn't. But there was nothing he could do about it, short of *demanding* that Jiterica put her suit back on. And he didn't have the right to do that.

Just then, someone else entered the room from the bathroom in the rear. It was Pfeffer, one of the ship's security officers.

"Paris," she said, acknowledging him.

The ensign put two and two together. "I guess you're Stave's security escort."

Pfeffer nodded. Then she took note of Jiterica and looked concerned. "Isn't that difficult for you to do?"

"She's not doing it," said Stave, with just a hint of a glance in Paris's direction. "*I* am."

Pfeffer looked impressed. "Really."

For a moment, they stood there—all four of them. Finally, it was Stave who broke the silence. "Unfortunately," he said, "I've got a tactical meeting in a few minutes. I ought to be going."

"Of course," said Jiterica. And she retrieved her suit.

As she slipped it back on, Paris saw the way Stave

looked at her. It almost made him drop the pretense of polite behavior and confront the Magnian.

Almost. But he managed to restrain himself.

"Thank you so much," Jiterica told Stave once she had closed up her suit.

"It was my pleasure," said the Magnian. And with a nod to Paris, he left Jiterica's quarters, Pfeffer trailing in his wake.

Paris waited until the door slid closed behind Stave. Then he turned to Jiterica and said, "We have to talk."

"All right," she said.

He sat her down and, as well as he could, explained what had happened and why it wasn't proper. And he also told her how he felt about it.

"You've got a right to do anything you want," he said. "Everyone does. But it's traditional, in a monogamous relationship, for both partners to keep their clothes on. I mean . . . unless they're alone. Or with each other."

With every qualification, he sounded increasingly ridiculous. But it *wasn't* ridiculous. It was something Jiterica needed to know if she was to continue living among humanoids.

She considered the advice for a moment, her ghostly features knotted in concentration. Then she said, "Are you certain about this?"

Paris straightened. "Of course."

"The reason I ask," said Jiterica, "is that I've seen others take their clothes off, with no apparent concern about my being there. Gerda, for instance."

Paris didn't get it. "Gerda took her clothes off . . . ?"

"I ran into her as she was returning to her quarters from the gym. I had expressed curiosity about her Klingon upbringing and she had promised to show me some artifacts."

"Oh. That's different. Gerda's a woman—a female."

"But I'm a female as well," Jiterica pointed out.

"Yes," said Paris, "that's the point. You're both females."

"Then it's acceptable for those of the same sex to disrobe in front of one another?"

"Exactly."

Jiterica frowned. "Was it improper, then, for me to undress in front of Mister Simenon?"

It took him a moment to realize what she was referring to. "No," he said, "not at all. Mister Simenon was helping you. He was making it easier for you to get around."

She looked at him. "But . . . so was Stave."

Paris sighed. "That's different. Stave had an interest in you that went beyond helping. He was . . . exploiting the situation."

Jiterica still looked uncomfortable. "It didn't seem that way to me. I thought he was being kind."

He knew he wasn't explaining very well. "Look," he said, "can you just trust me in this area?"

"Of course," she said. "I always trust you."

She did, too. And that placed a responsibility on him, which in turn compelled him to ask a question: *Am I telling Jiterica these things as a jealous lover, or as a friend who's concerned that she might be making a fool of herself?*

After all, some cultures preferred nudity in certain situations. Betazoids, for instance. And they were among the most enlightened species in the Federation.

"Listen," said Paris, "it's your decision. But if I were you, I wouldn't let Stave do that again."

Jiterica nodded. "All right. I won't."

But he could tell by the look on her ghostly face that she would never have made that choice on her own. She was embracing it strictly for his sake.

On one hand, Paris was pleased that Jiterica had trusted him as he had asked. But on the other, he wished she had reached her decision without him.

Sitting back in his chair, Picard considered the bizarre tale of Gary Mitchell, as compiled from the once-classified logs of the twenty-third-century *Starship Enterprise*.

As a first-year cadet at Starfleet Academy, Picard had studied Mitchell's transformation into a seemingly all-powerful being. However, in those days he wasn't motivated to examine every nuance of the fellow's behavior.

Not nearly as motivated as he was now.

But then, if all went as they hoped, Picard and his crew would be confronting an equally powerful being before long. They needed to secure any advantage they could. And if reading ship's logs might identify a weakness in Brakmaktin, the captain would go over them a thousand times.

It had already been a valuable exercise, reminding him of parts of the story he had forgotten—for instance, that Mitchell's increasing disdain for his colleagues had led to his telekinetic strangulation of a lieutenant named Lee Kelso at the lithium cracking station on Delta Vega.

Mitchell could have merely knocked Kelso unconscious and still kept him from acting as an inconvenience. However, he decided to murder the lieutenant instead.

Brakmaktin had displayed the same cold-blooded disregard for sentient life in dealing with his crewmates on the Nuyyad scout ship. According to the lone survivor, Brakmaktin hadn't hesitated or shown his victims any mercy. He had simply closed their throats, cutting off their air supply and asphyxiating them.

However, in Mitchell's case at least, there was still room for a more personal variety of punishment— something driven by vengeance rather than expedience. That much was clear in his dealings with James Kirk, Mitchell's captain.

According to the logs, Mitchell and Kirk had become friends at Starfleet Academy and worked together on two previous assignments before coming to the *Enterprise*. Kirk's logs reflected his affection and admiration for Mitchell, even when the latter seemed no longer to be himself.

Mitchell had no doubt started out with similar feelings about his captain. In fact, he had risked his life to save Kirk's at least once. And even after his exposure to the barrier energies, Mitchell seemed to harbor a certain respect for Kirk.

But in time, that respect turned into something else.

Resentment? Embarrassment? A need to dissociate himself from his past? It was hidden beneath a veneer of dispassion and indifference, but it was there nonetheless.

Why else would Mitchell have forced Kirk to bow down to him and lift his hands in supplication? Why would he have opened an empty grave at Kirk's feet, or created a headstone with the captain's name on it? Why else except for the fact that he still felt a kinship with Kirk, and hated himself for doing so?

Mitchell could have destroyed his old friend many times over, both on the *Enterprise* and on the barren surface of Delta Vega. But he had refrained. He had felt compelled to castigate Kirk rather than simply eliminate him.

And in the end, it cost him dearly, because it gave the captain an opportunity to enlist the other player in their little drama—Elizabeth Dehner, resident psychiatrist and budding superbeing in her own right.

Like Mitchell, Dehner had been suffused with the energies in the barrier, and had begun to evolve into something more powerful than *Homo sapiens*. But Mitchell was so impressed with himself, he didn't think twice about letting Dehner stand next to him as he humbled his friend Kirk.

Apparently, he hadn't entertained the possibility that Dehner would turn on him. But as Kirk was driven to his knees, he pointed out to Dehner that Mitchell would kill her as soon as she became a threat to him, spurring her to level an attack against Mitchell then and there.

The two mutated beings exchanged bolts of crackling blue energy until Dehner was near death. But her efforts had drained Mitchell, temporarily robbing him of his power.

Picard wished he had someone like Dehner to help him now. Unfortunately, even if she had survived, she would have become as bad a threat as Mitchell.

The captain would have to settle for the Magnians, the only other beings in the galaxy who enjoyed even a measure of barrier-enhanced power. Unfortunately, their combined mental abilities—impressive as they seemed to Picard and his crew—wouldn't be nearly the equal of Brakmaktin's.

By the time the *Stargazer* tracked the Nuyyad down, his power might well have grown beyond Mitchell's. It might have become something to which Mitchell could only aspire.

Would Brakmaktin have any weaknesses at all, by then? Say, the petty emotions Mitchell had displayed? Perhaps not.

But Picard had to grasp at the straws available to him. After all, knowledge was a kind of power as well, and if he was to even hope to succeed in his mission, he needed all the power he could get.

He closed his eyes and massaged the bridge of his nose. *And,* he added, *I need to stop thinking about Serenity.*

She had been hovering at the edge of his consciousness since he woke that morning. It was difficult for him knowing she was on the ship, yet having to maintain his distance from her.

No doubt, she felt the same way. However, she knew the magnitude of what they were up against as well as he did. Better, perhaps, in that she had powers of her own, and therefore a better sense of the damage Brakmaktin could inflict on an adversary.

Just then, the intercom system came alive. "Captain Picard?" said a familiar voice—that of Gerda Asmund.

He sat forward. "Yes?"

"Lieutenant Kastiigan and I have come up with a set of coordinates, sir. They're just under twenty light-years from our current position."

Only four days away, the captain thought. "Plot a course, Lieutenant."

"I already have," said Gerda.

He smiled. "I will advise our helm officer to pursue it. Good work, both of you."

"Thank you, sir," said Gerda. Kastiigan, who had remained silent to that point, echoed the sentiment.

Picard felt his jaw muscles ripple. They were getting closer to Brakmaktin. He could only hope they found him in time.

Chapter Six

PICARD COULDN'T HELP FEELING a wave of disappointment as he scrutinized his forward viewscreen. "These are the coordinates?" he asked.

"They are," Gerda told him.

He frowned. "You're certain?"

"Aye, sir," she said, a tinge of resentment in her voice.

And it was justified, the captain was forced to concede. After all, Gerda had never given him reason to doubt the accuracy of her reports.

But he had expected something more here, at the end of their light-years–long journey. Some debris perhaps, some lingering traces of radiation. But there wasn't any. In fact, there was no evidence whatsoever of a violent encounter between a Nuyyad scout and some other vessel.

Nothing but a scattering of stars on the void. And they weren't giving up anything Picard wanted to know.

He turned to Gerda. "See if you can find an ion trail."

"Aye, sir," said the navigation officer, and proceeded as the captain had asked.

Picard drummed his fingers on his armrest. Questions came to mind, the answers to which made him uneasy.

What if Gerda and Kastiigan had settled on the wrong set of coordinates? What if, in fact, the place they were looking for was light-years away—and they had wasted the last four days speeding here at warp nine point two?

No, Picard insisted. *Have a little faith.* There was no better navigator in the fleet than Gerda. If she believed this was the spot, then more than likely it *was.*

He watched his navigator initiate scan after scan, using one sensor modality after another. And when none of them turned anything up, she expanded her range.

Her scan radius grew from ten kilometers to twenty. To thirty. To forty. And still no sign of what they were looking for.

The captain resisted the urge to get up and pace. *We cannot have come all this way for nothing . . .*

Suddenly, Gerda straightened in her seat. "I've got something," she said.

"A trail?" Picard asked hopefully.

She confirmed it. "It's faint, but it's there. And there's no question it was made by a warp engine."

"What kind?" he pressed, wanting to get some idea of what they were up against.

That took a little longer. Finally, Gerda looked up from her console and said, "I'd say Yridian."

It was a common enough drive, at least in the construction of cargo haulers. *Good news,* the captain thought. Had the trail been left by a warship, they would have faced a more daunting task when they caught up with her.

It would be difficult enough to face Brakmaktin as it was. With a warship at his disposal, it might have been impossible.

"Shall I follow it?" asked Idun Asmund, who was manning the helm.

"By all means," said Picard.

Then he sat back in his center seat, drummed his fingertips on his armrest some more, and waited.

Pushing himself on his back along the Ubarrak access tube, Nikolas counted the tiny doors set into the metal surface above him until he got to the fifth one. Then he pressed his hand against the plate beside it and watched the door swing open, revealing a set of eight small studs within.

Four were black, two were red, and two were green. Using the thumb and forefinger of his right hand, he pressed the red studs at the same time. It was, as he had learned through painstaking study, the procedure for manually overriding the battle cruiser's helm controls and activating her starboard thrusters.

That is, if such an outcome wasn't made impossible by forces beyond Nikolas's control.

Indeed, nothing was happening—no growl of moving machine parts, no hiss of forced gas-cmission. Releasing the studs, he pressed them a second time. Still nothing.

Nikolas wasn't surprised. This was only the most recent in a long line of failures.

Previously, he had attempted to shut down the antimatter fuel injectors, sabotage the conduits that sent plasma flowing to the nacelles, and create a feedback wave in the power relays that would fry the warp coils. But nothing had worked. Controls had frozen, borrowed tools had stopped working, and backup systems had materialized where they hadn't existed before.

No matter what Nikolas did, the alien seemed to have anticipated it and come up with a way to prevent it. Which was why, many hours later, the cruiser's engines were still running and she hadn't diverged from her course by even a millimeter.

And yet, despite ample evidence of his meddling, the alien himself was nowhere to be seen. There were plenty of Ubarrak lying in the corridors and the lifts, staring into infinity until their bodies finally shut down from neglect. But no sign of the monster who had stricken them.

At first, Nikolas was glad he hadn't run into his nemesis, since his only chance was to act surreptitiously. Then he began to wonder. At one point, he even tried to locate the alien by accessing the internal sensor grid. However, the sensor logs didn't cooperate with him any better than the helm controls had, leaving Nikolas to draw his own conclusions.

And the most obvious one, hard as it was for him to understand, was that the alien had left the ship.

But that begged a question—if he wasn't on the cruiser, where was he? Certainly not on the *Iktoj'ni*, which was by far the warship's inferior when it came to speed and power—and that was *before* she got beat up.

Hadn't the alien made a comment to Nikolas about the Ubarrak ship being in good condition? Why would he have said that unless he planned to use her somehow? And why would he have gone to the trouble of transporting Nikolas over from the *Iktoj'ni* when it would have been so much easier just to kill him?

No, Nikolas thought, *the alien is here. He's got to be. It's just a matter of looking for him in the right place.*

And the human would do that—he would have to, because the world the alien had plucked from his mind was a populated one, with hundreds of thousands of Ubarrak mining dilithium in its crust. The alien couldn't be allowed to do to them what he had done to the crew of the warship.

His jaw clenching, Nikolas started pulling himself back down the access tube.

Picard rose from his center seat and moved forward toward the viewscreen, where Gerda had moments earlier established a visual of their objective.

It was an Yridian cargo ship, identifiable by her snub nose and her widely spaced nacelles. The captain had seen her like at starbases all across the sector, hauling everything from stem bolts to plasma manifolds.

But he had never seen one in this kind of shape. Judging by the savage burn marks decorating her hull, she had been raked by at least one energy barrage and possibly more.

And she wasn't under way. She was just hanging there in the void, her observation ports only dimly illuminated.

"Slow to impulse," Picard said.

"Aye, sir," said Idun, dropping the *Stargazer* out of warp.

"Mister Ben Zoma," said the captain, addressing the ship's intercom system, "report to the bridge, please."

"Aye, sir," came Ben Zoma's reply.

Picard tilted his head slightly as he regarded the cargo hauler. "Life signs?"

Gerda turned to him. "None, sir."

Picard frowned, unable to trust even in his sensors. For all he knew, Brakmaktin had foiled them somehow and was still ensconced on the cargo hauler, lying in wait for whoever came aboard.

Or he had moved on, and the vessel was as it appeared—empty of living occupants. There was only one way to tell.

Hearing the soft hiss of the turbolift doors, the captain glanced over his shoulder and saw Ben Zoma emerge from the compartment. Before he had gone very far, his eyes were drawn to the image of the cargo hauler.

"According to sensors," said Picard, "she's devoid of life. But given what we're dealing with . . ."

"It's hard to be sure," said Ben Zoma.

Picard turned to Gerda. "Transporter range?"

"At current speed," said the navigator, "slightly more than eighteen minutes."

"I am going to take a team," said Picard, "to see if I can shed any light on what happened there. You have the bridge in my absence, Gilaad."

Another first officer might have reminded the captain that he was too valuable a commodity to include on an away team. But Ben Zoma had known Picard long enough to know his protest would fall on deaf ears.

So all he did was give Picard a look and say, "I'll let Dojjaron and Santana know to stand by."

As the captain went aft, he passed Kastiigan at the science station. The Kandilkari looked up, no doubt hoping to be brought along. After all, he had been requesting to take on hazardous assignments for some time.

Briefly, Picard considered the idea of granting Kastiigan's wish. But by the time he reached the turbolift, he had come to think better of it.

They were dealing with a most unusual being in Brakmaktin—one who not only was powerful, but had the finely honed adversarial instincts of the Nuyyad. Under the circumstances, it seemed like a better idea to take a team composed exclusively of security officers. Then, if something went wrong, they would be better equipped to respond.

Sorry, Lieutenant, Picard thought, *perhaps another time.* And as the turbolift doors opened, he left the bridge.

As Nikolas made his way through the Ubarrak ship's symbol-incised corridors, he got a strong feeling of déjà vu—as if he had conducted such a search before.

I have, it occurred to him. *In my dream.* But then, he had been searching for his friend Locklear. Now he was looking for the alien who had brought him there . . .

Brakmaktin.

Nikolas stopped in his tracks, a chill climbing his spine. The alien had never mentioned his name, and Nikolas hadn't asked. But somehow he *knew* it.

Brakmaktin. And he came from a world of wide, cracked plains and clouds of volcanic smoke.

And he hadn't always been this way—a being of power with shining, silver eyes. Not long ago he was a simple technician, no more fearsome than any other member of his species.

How do I know all this? Nikolas asked himself. Was it possible that when the alien scoured out his consciousness, he left a little of his own behind?

This way, he thought.

Then he realized that it wasn't his thought at all. It had come to him unbidden, the product of a consciousness other than his own. And strangest of all, he knew which way *this way* was.

He continued down the corridor he was already following, then made a turn to the left that brought him to a lift. Taking it two decks down, he exited and turned to his right this time.

It was a deck he hadn't yet had occasion to visit. In fact, he realized as if only now awakening from a dream, it might have been the only one in that category. And the more he thought about it, the less he believed it was a coincidence.

At the end of the corridor, he turned left again and came to a set of doors. They opened at his approach, revealing a large room that had once been the cruiser's armory.

Its walls were covered with rows of disruptor weapons, short-barreled pistols as well as vicious-looking rifles. Once, it seemed to Nikolas, the Ubarrak must have enjoyed easy access to all the ordnance they kept there.

But that was before Brakmaktin had transformed the place into a fully realized cavern full of mineral pillars, not unlike the ones Nikolas had encountered on the *Iktoj'ni*. But far from taking the alien days to create, it had taken him less than a dozen hours. Clearly, he was getting more practiced at it.

As for Brakmaktin himself, he was floating in the center of the room a good half meter above the deck—eyes closed, feet together, massive arms extended sideways.

But he looked different from the last time Nikolas

had seen him. His fringe of lank dark hair had turned silver, almost as silver as his eyes.

"Levitation," said the alien, as if to no one in particular, "is a simple matter once you understand the workings of gravity. As simple as shaping a lesser being's thoughts."

Nikolas frowned. *Which explains why I never ran into him.*

Abruptly, Brakmaktin turned his eyes on the human. "I've made changes," he noted.

"Yes," the human said drily. "I can see that."

Brakmaktin glared at him, clearly not pleased with the sarcasm. Then, by degrees, his expression softened.

"In any case," he said, "it is only a temporary measure. When we reach our destination, I will create something more complete. More satisfying."

Nikolas couldn't imagine what the alien would do when he reached the Ubarrak world. He didn't *want* to imagine it. It was bound to be horrific, worse than anything he had seen so far.

He couldn't let it happen. He had to stop it—if not by bringing the ship about, then by bringing *Brakmaktin* about.

"You don't want to go where we're headed," Nikolas said.

"But I do," the alien told him offhandedly.

"You can't," said Nikolas. His mind raced to come up with a reason. "Its atmosphere's been poisoned . . . by experimentation with biogenic weapons."

Brakmaktin looked at him, his head tilted to the

side. "There was no mention of that in your vessel's database. Or the database in this vessel, either."

He checked the databases? He's more thorough than I thought. "It happened recently," Nikolas said.

The alien continued to stare at him for a moment. Then he said, "You're lying."

And before Nikolas knew it, he was flying backward across the room, headed for the bulkhead behind him.

Don't tense up, he told himself.

And he didn't. But it still sent shoots of pain through his bones when he smashed into the mineral-encrusted bulkhead, and again when he plummeted to the metal deck.

Tasting blood, Nikolas looked up at Brakmaktin. The alien was still eyeing him from the center of the room, his eyes glowing with a fierce silver light.

Brakmaktin had the power to kill him with a gesture. Both Nikolas and his tormentor knew that. And for a moment, Nikolas thought that Brakmaktin would do it.

Then the alien turned away, as if Nikolas no longer interested him. The human breathed a sigh of relief.

But he didn't understand Brakmaktin's restraint. Why had he kept Nikolas around in the first place? Why was he *continuing* to keep him around?

Did he think that Nikolas had something he needed—some hard-to-get information about Ubarrak space, maybe? Or did the alien just want some company as he moved to meet his objective, whatever that might be?

Clearly, Brakmaktin could read Nikolas's thoughts. But if he had "heard" the question in the human's mind, he didn't seem the least bit inclined to answer it. He just hung there in defiance of the ship's artificial gravity . . .

And everything else in the universe.

Chapter Seven

PICARD MATERIALIZED in a centrally located corridor of the cargo hauler along with Joseph, Pierzynski, Pfeffer, and Iulus, all five of them wearing Starfleet environmental suits.

The garments were meant to protect them against radiation, extremes of heat and cold, and airlessness. However, they might not be of much use if Brakmaktin had set a trap for them.

Once the captain's team was all accounted for, he cast a glance in either direction. The corridor was empty. But then, Refsland, the transporter operator, had made sure they wouldn't appear in a location likely to present problems.

According to Refsland, a number of corridors and compartments were filled with "formations," though he couldn't say exactly what they were. Before Picard and his team were through, he intended to answer that question.

Among others.

"Mister Joseph," he said, "take Lieutenants Pfeffer and Iulus, and check the engine room and the lower decks. Mister Pierzynski, you are with me."

The *Stargazer*'s sensor scans had shown them where the ship's lifts were. While the captain and Pierzynski set off in one direction, Joseph's group went in the other.

Picard and Pierzynski found a lift station just where it was supposed to be. Getting inside, they punched in a destination and made their ascent to the ship's bridge level.

When the lift doors opened, they emerged and looked around. The captain hadn't known what he would find, but he certainly hadn't expected *this*.

The corridor was filled with a forest of hourglass-shaped shafts connecting the deck below with the ceiling above, and everything—bulkheads included—was covered with a slick orange-and-blue veneer. If Picard hadn't known better, he would have said he was surrounded by mineral deposits, the sort one might encounter in a subterranean chamber.

A quick tricorder scan showed him that it was true—they *were* mineral deposits. *Formations,* Refsland had called them. Now the captain understood what his transporter operator had been talking about.

Turning sideways, he slid between two of the shafts and made his way in the direction of the bridge. With a muttered curse, Pierzynski followed. In a matter of moments, they reached the set of doors they were looking for.

When Picard laid his hand on the bulkhead plate, the doors slid open—and released a puff of gray smoke. Exchanging glances with Pierzynski, the captain went inside.

He found plenty of support there for the notion that the ship had been through a battle. One of the control consoles had been thoroughly blackened, an exposed data conduit was still spewing sparks, and a break in an EPS line was causing the overheads to strobe insanely.

What Picard did *not* find was even a hint of captain and crew. That puzzled him. If they had perished in the battle, their bodies should have been sprawled there.

They had been removed, probably by Brakmaktin. But for what purpose? And was it before the battle or after?

And while he was on the subject, with whom had the cargo hauler clashed? If Brakmaktin wasn't to be found there any longer, they would need to identify his means of escape.

"Mister Pierzynski," he said, "download the sensor logs—internal as well as external."

"Aye, sir," said the security officer.

Picard looked around the bridge. Next to the center seat, he saw a dark stain on the carpet. Kneeling, he scanned it with his tricorder, which identified it as blood—the Vobilite variety, shed between two and three days earlier.

He wasn't sure what to make of it. Had Brakmaktin caused the injury, or was that the work of whoever had left his claw marks on the hull? Had the Nuyyad even been on board at the time, or had he arrived later on?

"Captain?" said Pierzynski.

Picard turned to him—and saw by his expression that the security officer was less than pleased with the results of his effort. "Problem, Lieutenant?"

"I'm afraid so, sir. The sensor logs have been wiped. There's not even a shred of data left in them."

The captain looked at him. "You mean they were damaged?"

Pierzynski shook his head. "No, sir. *Erased.*"

"I see," said Picard.

So Brakmaktin was covering his trail. That meant it would be difficult to take him by surprise.

"See if you can access anything at all," said the captain. "Even if it is only a record of repairs."

"Aye, sir," Pierzynski said, and bent to his task.

In the meantime, Picard contacted Ben Zoma and described the situation. "I would like to speak with Dojjaron," he added, speaking into the communicator grid that was part of his helmet. "Perhaps he can tell me about those shafts out in the corridor."

"Acknowledged," said the first officer. "I'll have Cadwallader patch you through."

A few moments later, Picard heard the jangling voice of the foremost elder. "What is it?"

The captain told him about the mineral deposits. "Any idea what they might be?"

Dojjaron made a sound deep in his throat. "Brakmaktin is re-creating the safe-cavern of his clan. He'll need it if he's to produce young ones."

Picard absorbed the information. "Our sensors tell us he is no longer on this vessel. Having created such an environment, would he leave it behind?"

"Of course—because he can't complete his labors in the confines of a ship. There is more to creating a safe-cavern than fabricating a few mineral columns. He needs more space in which to work—and he won't stop until he finds it."

"Then why create the mineral deposits at all?" the captain asked. "Was he merely exploring the extent of his abilities?"

"That," said Dojjaron, "is a question for Brakmaktin."

Picard understood. Until then, no Nuyyad had ever had the option of manufacturing his own safe-cavern. It was difficult for even Dojjaron to explain Brakmaktin's behavior.

"Thank you," said Picard, and terminated the link. Then he contacted Joseph and asked for a progress report.

"I've never seen anything like it, sir," said the security officer. "The engine room's been transformed into a cave. Not just made to look like one—I mean actually *turned into* one. And the warp reactor . . . you can barely see it, it's so caked over."

The captain sympathized with Joseph's reaction. "We encountered the same sort of environment in the vicinity of the bridge. Continue your investigation, Lieutenant—and if you come across even the slightest indication that Brakmaktin is aboard, let me know immediately."

"I will, sir," Joseph promised.

Picard knew his acting security chief would exercise the utmost care. But he knew also that if Brakmaktin wanted to remain undetected, he could probably do so.

After all, he was powerful enough to turn an engine room into a cave. What would stop him from getting into an adversary's head and creating a convenient illusion?

The captain looked around the bridge. It appeared empty but for Pierzynski and himself. Yet Brakmaktin could have been standing right next to him, watching him, biding his time . . .

The thought made the hairs on the back of the captain's neck stand up. Placing his back against a bulkhead, he put his hand on his phaser and waited for Pierzynski to finish his work.

One thing was certain: Santana had been telling the truth about Brakmaktin and his superior abilities. What had happened on the *Iktoj'ni* was ample proof of it.

Nikolas hadn't intended to relocate the bodies of the Ubarrak as he had relocated his crewmates on the *Iktoj'ni*. The Ubarrak weren't dead, so it didn't seem right to lay them side by side in a cargo hold. But the more he saw of them, the harder it was to leave them where they were.

Finally, he couldn't stand it any longer. Hefting an Ubarrak onto his shoulder, Nikolas lugged him into a lift and brought him down to a mess hall he had discovered in his travels.

By the time he came back for a second one, winded and perspiring because Ubarrak were so much heavier than humans, Brakmaktin had made himself comfortable on the bridge. He was sitting in the center seat, surrounded by an entourage of half-formed mineral pillars, and staring at the viewscreen.

All it showed were the stars streaming past. However, Nikolas allowed for the possibility that Brakmaktin saw more in what was on the screen than he did. Or maybe the alien didn't see anything at all—it was hard to say.

And Brakmaktin wasn't exactly a font of information. In fact, he was no more talkative than the Ubarrak whose intellects he had so casually erased.

Nikolas had seen species that were violent by nature—the Klingons, for instance—and those that killed without quarter. But he had never seen anyone sit in the midst of the fallen and act as if they weren't there.

Swearing softly, the human planted himself by another of Brakmaktin's victims and hooked his hands under the fellow's armpits. He was about to drag the Ubarrak to his feet when the poor bastard began to tremble.

Before Nikolas knew it, the trembling evolved into a series of jerks, the Ubarrak's head pounding the deck as if he were trying to free himself from his benefactor's grasp. Though the Ubarrak was brain-dead already, Nikolas couldn't let him smash his skull to pulp. Slipping beneath the Ubarrak's head, Nikolas held on to him and absorbed the impacts as best he could.

As it turned out, they didn't last that much longer. A minute at most. Then the Ubarrak just went limp in Nikolas's arms.

The human pressed his fingers against an artery in the Ubarrak's neck, feeling for a pulse. There wasn't any. The Ubarrak wasn't just brain-dead anymore—he was dead altogether.

And Brakmaktin continued to sit there with his back to them, staring at his screen.

Something snapped in Nikolas then—not just because of what had happened there on the battle cruiser, or even what had happened on the *Iktoj'ni*. It was because of what *hadn't* happened.

Sliding the Ubarrak off him, Nikolas came forward and planted himself in front of Brakmaktin, blocking his view of the screen. The alien looked at him, his eyes moving almost imperceptibly, but he didn't say anything. Being a telepath, he may have believed he didn't have to.

But Nikolas wasn't a mind reader. He wanted—needed—to ask his questions out loud.

"You destroyed everyone except me," he spat, his eyes as hot as coals in their sockets. "Why?"

The alien remained silent, his features as immobile as those of a stone sculpture.

Nikolas grabbed the console that separated them and leaned forward until his face was centimeters from Brakmaktin's. "What do you need me for?"

Again, no answer was forthcoming.

"Why do you keep me around?" the human demanded, his voice taut and strained.

Still no response.

"There has to be a reason," he insisted.

If there was, Brakmaktin didn't seem inclined to share it with him.

Consumed by anger and frustration, Nikolas did something he wouldn't have done in a calmer and wiser state—he pounded his fists on the console, daring the alien to take offense.

But Brakmaktin still refused to acknowledge him. He just went on staring as if Nikolas weren't there.

No, the human resolved. *You're not going to get away with that. Not anymore.*

He didn't care what Brakmaktin did to him. He just wanted to wipe that condescending expression off the alien's ugly face.

"You know what I think?" he said, his voice ringing from one end of the bridge to the other. "I think you're scared. I think you look out at the universe and all you see is not-you, and it scares the living hell out of you."

The alien made a sound he no doubt intended as a gesture of dismissal. But Nikolas heard something in it that told him he was on the right track.

"And you need someone like me," he went on, "to remind you what it was like to be just Brakmaktin— before he gained all his power and became someone else."

The alien's nostrils flared, but the rest of him

remained as it was. And Nikolas couldn't stand that.

"Go ahead," he snapped in Brakmaktin's face, "prove I'm wrong, dammit! Destroy me!"

The words were out before he realized how stupid he was to utter them. What was he trying to accomplish—other than getting himself killed, maybe?

But somehow, he didn't feel that he was in any jeopardy. He felt that he was right. And if that was so, Brakmaktin wouldn't kill him any more than he would kill himself.

The monster glared at him with his silver orbs, his brow ledge lowered in restrained fury. *Destroy me*, he echoed ominously in the human's mind.

And for just a second, Nikolas's blood ran cold, because he thought Brakmaktin might actually do it. Then the alien turned away, as if he were no longer interested in the topic.

But it wasn't lack of interest. It was shame, because Nikolas had violated his superiority and his solitude, all in one fell swoop, and Brakmaktin hadn't been able to do anything about it.

Just the way Nikolas felt when the alien pulled out his deepest memories.

He eyed Brakmaktin a moment longer. Then he walked away on his own terms, and found another Ubarrak who needed his attention. With an effort, he slung the fellow over his shoulder and made his way to the lift.

And somehow it seemed easier now than before. But then, Nikolas had won this battle, despite all of Brakmaktin's power. He had come out on top.

As to whether that would be worth something at any point . . . he could only hope.

Pierzynski had just finished downloading the last bit of data he could find when Picard received a call from Pug Joseph.

"Go ahead," said the captain.

"I'm in the main cargo bay, sir, and I can see what happened to the crew—or most of it. There are maybe fifty of them down here, lying side by side in two neat rows. Whoever did this must have cared about them."

That wasn't Brakmaktin, surely, thought Picard. Then who could it have been? And where was that individual now—lying dead somewhere himself?

"Remain there," he told Joseph. "Mister Pierzynski and I will join you momentarily." He felt compelled to see the scene in the cargo bay with his own eyes.

Then, as expeditiously as they could, they would comb the parts of the ship they hadn't gotten to yet. Eventually, they would come across the crewman who had laid his comrades out in such dignified fashion.

But they wouldn't know that it was he who had done it. He would appear to be just another corpse, and the mystery surrounding his actions would go unsolved.

The captain wished he could stay and try to puzzle it all out. However, he had a significantly more important job to do, and time was precious.

The seventh or eighth time Nikolas went to the bridge to pick up an Ubarrak, he saw that the image on the viewscreen had changed. No longer filled with a river of stars, it displayed an M-class planet with all the trimmings.

Blue oceans. Green and brown land masses. Cloud cover. Polar icecaps. The works.

And a population too, though it wasn't native to that world. It had been brought there generations earlier to reap a harvest of dilithium, which the Ubarrak—like the Federation—used to control the matter-antimatter reactions in their warp drives.

Nikolas knew about this world because it was the one Brakmaktin had pulled from his mind. He hadn't expected to see it so soon, since it was still a light-year too distant for the warship's sensors to pick up. However, as the alien had already demonstrated, he could do things others could not.

He had had but one deficiency, and that was his lack of knowledge of this galaxy. But thanks to Nikolas, that deficiency was no more. Brakmaktin had been able to find whatever he needed in the human's defenseless mind.

Had he restricted himself to the databases on the *Iktoj'ni* and the battle cruiser, he could have gotten more information than Nikolas could ever give him. But it was easier for him to reach into Nikolas's mind for it.

And more fun too. That was clear from the expression he had seen on Brakmaktin's face. It had definitely been more entertaining to rummage through a brain than a computer memory.

Nikolas wished he could press a reset button and make everything the way it was before he left the

Stargazer. He wished he could be back there now with Obal and all the others—even Paris, who had begun to open up to him a little.

He wished that he had never heard of Brakmaktin or the Nuyyad or the Ubarrak ship they were on, or the world they were headed for. But most of all, he wished he knew of a way to stop his monster of a companion before he killed anyone else.

"No," said Brakmaktin. "That is not what you want most."

Nikolas turned to him. He could tell by the alien's expression that he had been reading Nikolas's thoughts.

"I can grant your wishes," said Brakmaktin. "Can . . . and will. But only one. The one you desire above all the rest."

Nikolas wondered which wish that was, but only for a moment. Then, as the answer dawned on him, he got the feeling that there was someone standing behind him.

No, he thought. *It's not possible . . .*

Whirling, he saw the woman he thought he would never see again. The woman he loved. The woman who had come from another universe and returned to it the same way, taking his every possibility of happiness with her.

Gerda Idun.

Nikolas shook his head. Brakmaktin was powerful, but he couldn't reach across the barriers separating one dimension from the next. No one could.

Still, it was Gerda Idun standing in front of him, exactly as he remembered her, wearing the same gray leather vest and boots in which she had first transported onto the *Stargazer.*

But how *could* it be her? She had gone back where she came from, to a universe where humanity was fighting for its life against an alliance of Klingons and Cardassians.

He knew that with a certainty. And yet, he couldn't help drinking in the sight of her.

"Andreas," she said, in a voice that was unmistakably *hers.* Her brow furrowed. "I've missed you . . ."

Nikolas felt a tingle travel the length of his spine. Despite what he knew, he wanted Gerda Idun to be real—wanted it as he had never wanted anything in his life.

Crossing the bridge, he approached her. And the closer he got, the more obvious it became that she *was* real—a being made of flesh and blood, just like Nikolas himself.

Not an illusion or a dream. A reality.

Stopping in front of her, he looked into her sea-blue eyes. They were real, too. And he couldn't deny the spark of intelligence that resided in them.

"Andreas," she said again, and smiled. Then she brushed his hand with her own.

He reached for her fingers, to intertwine them with his. "It's me," he confirmed. "But how—?"

Before he finished getting the words out, he realized that something was wrong. Gerda Idun was fading, becoming unsubstantial. He grabbed at her hand but felt nothing there.

"What's happening?" she asked, dread and disappointment mingling in her tone.

Nikolas didn't know. But then, he didn't know how she had gotten there in the first place.

"No!" he insisted. He turned to Brakmaktin, heat rising in his face. "No, dammit!"

But it didn't help. When he turned back to Gerda Idun, she was airier and more poorly defined than a hologram.

"Stop!" he shouted, as if he could will her into existence as Brakmaktin had. "Come back!"

She kept fading, though, eluding his attempts to make her whole. And in a heartbeat, she was gone altogether.

Nikolas whimpered like a dog. She had *been* there. He had *felt* her. It wasn't an illusion—it was *her.*

And now she was gone again, returned to whatever place Brakmaktin had plucked her from—wondering how she had seen Nikolas again when that was impossible, and what it all meant.

He slumped against a bulkhead, feeling desolate, hollowed out. It was even worse than the first time he had lost her. And then it occurred to him—that was *exactly* what Brakmaktin had intended.

Darting a glance at the alien, he saw that he was right. Brakmaktin was studying his misery with a certain satisfaction—the kind a child might take from crushing an ant.

Destroy me, the alien said in Nikolas's mind.

He was taking his revenge for what the human had said about Brakmaktin needing him, cruelly reminding Nikolas of who had power over whom.

Like a child, the human thought again. *A petty, irrational child.*

For a while, it had seemed that Brakmaktin was growing more distant, more aloof. Not anymore. Now he was becoming the kind of being who derived pleasure from the pain of others.

And that made him more dangerous to everyone alive.

Chapter Eight

PICARD STOOD IN THE *Iktoj'ni*'s main cargo bay and surveyed the corpses laid out before him. *Joseph was right,* he told himself. They could only have been assembled this way by someone who cared about them.

The away team had discovered fifteen other corpses scattered about the ship, either in their quarters or elsewhere—three in the mess hall, three more in the cargo hauler's modest sickbay, and one in a turbolift.

Picard had opted to leave them where he and his officers found them. Unlike the individual who had transported so many of his friends to the cargo bay, the captain didn't have the time to perform such services.

As for Brakmaktin . . . if he was hiding, he had done a superlative job of it. It seemed more likely to Picard that the alien had left the *Iktoj'ni* on the vessel that attacked her, exchanging ships as he had done with the scout.

"Mister Ben Zoma," the captain said, again employing the com device in his helmet.

"Aye, sir," said the first officer. "Ready to beam out?"

Picard was about to reply in the affirmative when Pierzynski said, "Hang on, sir. Something doesn't jibe."

The security officer was studying his tricorder, a look of consternation on his face. The captain asked Ben Zoma to stand by, then moved to Pierzynski's side and took a look.

"This is the crew manifest," said Pierzynski. "I downloaded it when we were up on the bridge. There are fifty-nine names here. But we've only accounted for fifty-eight bodies."

"We could have missed one," said Iulus.

Joseph shook his head inside his helmet. "I don't think so. We were pretty thorough."

"Even if we have overlooked someone," Picard observed, "there is nothing left for us to accomplish here. We need to return to the *Stargazer*."

But before he had finished, he saw Pierzynski's eyes open with surprise. "This can't be right," the officer muttered.

"Lieutenant?" said Picard.

Looking up at him, Pierzynski handed over his tricorder. Its screen showed the captain a column of names.

And the one at the top was *Andreas Nikolas*.

It wasn't exactly a common name. And though Picard didn't know what had become of the ensign after he left the *Stargazer,* it wasn't unusual for those who left the fleet to turn to commercial shipping as an alternative.

But everyone on the away team had known Nikolas. If they had come across him, they would have known it—and said something.

Which meant they hadn't seen him in the course of their search. And as Pierzynski had pointed out, they *were* a body short . . .

A body who could have carried thirty-three others there to the cargo bay and arranged them on the deck. Nikolas was a good friend—he had demonstrated that on the *Stargazer.* If his comrades had perished and he was the only survivor, he would certainly have done what he could for them.

A drop of ice water collected in the small of Picard's back. Was that it—the solution to the mystery of how the bodies had gotten there? But if it was, it raised more questions than it answered.

For instance, how had Nikolas survived when the others had not? And if he wasn't on the ship, a corpse among all the other corpses, where in blazes *was* he?

"Captain?" said Ben Zoma over the com link.

Picard licked his lips. Was it possible that when Brakmaktin left the *Iktoj'ni,* he had taken Nikolas with him? Why would the Nuyyad have done that? What could he have gained by it?

The captain tried to figure it out. Unfortunately, none of the answers he came up with were happy ones.

"Sir?" Ben Zoma said, his tone noticeably more urgent this time.

"I am here, Gilaad," Picard assured him. He looked around at his companions, addressing them at the same time. "And you will be surprised to hear what we have discovered. . . ."

Nikolas was sitting in the Ubarrak mess hall among the fourteen Ubarrak he had carried or dragged there, eating something that reminded him of fresh mahogany shavings and curdled milk, when he heard words slither through his brain: *There's a squadron coming to meet us.*

Though the advisory wasn't accompanied by a voice per se, there was no doubt in his mind where it came from. Or why.

For the better part of a second, Nikolas considered remaining where he was. After all, he wasn't in a position to change the outcome of what was going to happen. Why give the alien the satisfaction of seeing his horror?

But he didn't know how Brakmaktin would react if he stayed where he was. He might cut an even broader swath of destruction out of resentment. *No,* Nikolas thought with bitter resolve, *it's better to go up to the bridge and take my punishment.* That way, others might not have to.

Pushing his chair out, he left the mess hall and made his way through a sea of mineral deposits to a lift. In a matter of moments, he had reached the bridge level, and in a few more he came out onto the bridge.

Beyond the silhouette of the alien and his attendant projections, the viewscreen was filled to its limits by the visage of an Ubarrak captain. He was thick-necked even for someone of his species, his slitted yellow eyes blazing with impatience in the cavernous sockets defined by his brow ridges.

"I repeat," he rasped, "this is Commander Goshevik of the Tenth System Defense Fleet. Come to an immediate halt, disengage your engines, and prepare to be boarded. Otherwise, you will be destroyed."

Of course, the battle cruiser hadn't communicated her business in advance. That would naturally make her the object of concern, if not outright suspicion.

And Brakmaktin didn't do a thing to allay it. He just stood there watching the screen—entertained, no doubt, by the seriousness of the Ubarrak's warning.

Nikolas guessed that the visual communication was only one-way. Had Goshevik been able to see who was manning the bridge of the battle cruiser, he would certainly have fired already instead of persisting in his warnings.

As it was, his patience seemed to be coming to an end, if the lowering of his brow ridge was any indication. "This is your last warning," Goshevik croaked officiously. "Disengage your engines or die."

Brakmaktin laughed harshly, neither replying nor altering the cruiser's course.

Abruptly, Goshevik's face vanished from the screen, to be replaced by an image of three state-of-the-art warships. Each was as big and powerful as the one Brakmaktin had commandeered.

And they would be in the defenders' weapons range at any moment. But Brakmaktin didn't seem deterred in the least. In fact, he appeared to be looking forward to the encounter.

Nikolas knew better than to counsel him to turn back. The alien hadn't heeded his advice before. It was unlikely that he would start doing so now.

Suddenly, the viewscreen was crammed full of azure light. Obviously, the Ubarrak had had enough.

Nikolas grabbed the console beside him and braced himself, wondering how much time would elapse before he felt the impact. *Not much,* he thought. And he was right.

He was jerked off his feet and slammed to the deck, reopening the cut above his eye. When he raised his head and got his bearings, he saw that a control console had exploded and was spraying hot, red sparks.

As he started to get up, the ship was rocked by a second volley, and then a third. An emergency siren went off as if the ship were crying out in pain.

Nikolas was surprised. Back on the *Iktoj'ni,* Brakmaktin hadn't let matters go so far. He had fended off the Ubarrak's first volley and then made sure they didn't release a second one.

It made the human wonder what was different this time. Was Brakmaktin allowing the cruiser to absorb this punishment for a reason? Or had he somehow underestimated the power the Ubarrak would bring against him?

As the viewscreen cleared, Nikolas saw the defenders wheel and come back for another pass. As before, a ball of blue radiance grew as it pursued them. Then the deck bucked once, twice, and again, and a second console erupted.

Nikolas had been in battles before, and had always hoped like hell that his ship would come out on top. It wasn't just a matter of wanting to survive. He had always believed that Starfleet was the side of the good guys.

But this time, Starfleet wasn't part of the equation. He was on an enemy ship, chained to a madman who had more power than anyone Nikolas had ever known.

More than anything else, Nikolas wanted the Ubarrak to tear them apart—to destroy the warship and pound Brakmaktin into subatomic particles. And if that meant Nikolas's dying as well, he had no problem with that.

It was a damned sight better than living with the knowledge that he had led Brakmaktin there.

He had barely completed the thought when the defenders reeled off another barrage. Nikolas was whipped in one direction and then the other, finally winding up at the base of a bulkhead with his side throbbing and blood trickling down the side of his face.

Peering through the thickening swirls of smoke, he caught a glimpse of Brakmaktin. The alien was standing just where he had been standing before, unmoved in every sense of the word.

But the battle cruiser had taken a beating, and Nikolas didn't have to consult a damage report to know she couldn't take much more. *Maybe it'll end here after all,* he thought.

Then Nikolas saw Brakmaktin raise his meaty hands and turn his palms toward the viewscreen, and heard the alien utter a single syllable: *"No!"*

It wasn't spoken loudly or even insistently, but the bridge echoed with it as if it were a thunderclap. And by the time the echoes died down, the pounding had stopped.

The bridge was peaceful again, tranquil, serene. The only sounds that marred the stillness were the soft trills of the surviving consoles.

Nikolas felt an urge to know what the alien had done, but he suppressed it. He was afraid of the answer.

Unfortunately for him, he got it anyway. "Look," said Brakmaktin, a savage urgency in his voice, and pushed the human toward the navigation panel with the power of his mind.

Each of the panel's monitors showed Nikolas a different battle cruiser—one of the three flying under Commander Goshevik's aegis. They were bristling with weaponry, their batteries pumping bright packets of destructive energy into the eternal night.

But if Goshevik's battle cruisers were still firing, why couldn't Nikolas feel it? Had his alien companion simply dampened the force of their attacks?

"This is what these ships looked like a minute ago," said Brakmaktin, answering the human's unspoken question. "And here is what they look like now."

Suddenly, the images changed. The battle cruisers

had become so much floating slag. And the Ubarrak who had operated them were nowhere to be seen.

Nikolas felt his breath catch in his throat. He hoped the crews of those ships had had time to escape in pods, to save themselves. But he didn't believe it—not for a moment.

Out of the corner of his eye, he saw Brakmaktin turn to him. He looked up, bracing himself for the alien's insufferable leer of triumph. But that's not what he saw.

Brakmaktin looked as if he was in some kind of pain. His cruel, shapeless mouth worked for a moment, as if he couldn't get it around the words he wanted to say. Finally, in a voice edged with misery, he said, "It is *wrong* . . ."

And then he disappeared.

Picard was still pondering what he had learned about Nikolas as he materialized on the transporter platform.

Eager to breathe the fresher air generated by the *Stargazer*'s life support systems, he removed his helmet. At the same time, the doors to the room opened and admitted Ben Zoma.

His expression indicated that he had something to report. "What is it?" the captain asked as he stepped down.

"Gerda's found another ion trail."

"Excellent," said Picard.

"That's the good news," said the first officer. "The bad is that it leads us in a considerably more interesting direction than the last trail we followed."

Picard looked at his first officer. *"How* interesting?"

"If we follow it long enough, it'll land us right in the middle of Ubarrak territory."

The captain recalled what Dojjaron had said about Brakmaktin, and how the "aberration" would need more room to create his safe-cavern. Apparently, he meant to find it among the hundreds of worlds ruled by the Ubarrak.

The *Stargazer* wasn't welcome in that part of space—not while the Ubarrak and the Federation were at odds with each other. If Picard tried to follow the ion trail, he would almost certainly end up being fired upon.

Hell, he might start a war. He could imagine what McAteer would say about *that.*

Of course, he had another option—he could leave the matter in the laps of the Ubarrak. They were, after all, the cause of countless Starfleet fatalities over the years.

But he knew he couldn't abandon his mission. He had to see it through to its end—not only for the sake of the Federation, but for that of the galaxy.

And for Nikolas's sake as well, if he was in truth Brakmaktin's prisoner.

"What do you think?" asked Ben Zoma.

"I think we should follow the trail," said Picard, "and hope we get to Brakmaktin before the Ubarrak get to *us.*"

"And that discovery you said would surprise me?"

"We will discuss it in my ready room."

*   *   *

This time, Nikolas didn't have to look very far to track down Brakmaktin. He was in the armory where the human had found him the first time.

But he wasn't suspended in midair, luxuriating in his power. He was standing in a corner, his head hanging, the side of his fist resting against the veneer-covered bulkhead.

"Get out," he jangled.

But it wasn't with any real conviction. And if Brakmaktin had truly wished to be rid of Nikolas, he could have made that happen easily enough.

I don't get it, Nikolas thought. *A moment ago, he was slaughtering Ubarrak without a second thought. Now he's standing in the corner like a mopey kid.*

Suddenly, the alien turned to look back at him. *He heard me,* Nikolas realized, and wondered stoically what price Brakmaktin would exact for his insubordination.

But the alien didn't lash out at him. He just gave him that pained look again, as if he were a child lost in a very deep and gloomy part of the forest.

"It is wrong," he said again, and this time his voice was different as well—quieter and slower, as if he were thinking even as he was speaking. "It is an aberration."

"What is?" Nikolas ventured.

Brakmaktin's silver eyes narrowed. *"I* am. And any offspring who issue from me."

Nikolas didn't understand. Was the alien feeling sorry for himself? How was that possible when he had the power to do anything he wanted?

"You're right," said Brakmaktin. "You don't understand." And he inserted the explanation into the human's mind—as well as a great deal more.

Nikolas had been wrong about where Brakmaktin came from. He wasn't part of the invasion force that had penetrated Federation space—the one the *Iktoj'ni* had been warned about.

He was a member of a species called Nuyyad, whose name sounded oddly familiar to Nikolas. But where had he heard it?

Then he remembered. The Nuyyad was the species Captain Picard had encountered on the other side of the galactic barrier. Nikolas wasn't serving on the *Stargazer* yet at the time, but he had read about the mission shortly after he came aboard.

The Nuyyad were aggressors, conquerors. And they had had their sights set on the Federation—apparently, even after the *Stargazer* crippled their preparations for an invasion.

Brakmaktin had been part of a scouting expedition—an attempt to gauge the strength and scope of the Federation, so the Nuyyad could strike without delay once they had replaced the depot the starship had destroyed.

But a portion of the vessel's shielding had gone down at a critical moment. Brakmaktin had been exposed to the barrier's energies, transformed into something that grew more insanely powerful by the moment.

The barrier, Nikolas thought. Of course.

Why hadn't he thought of it before, when he was

trying to decide if the alien could have been as powerful as those legendary superbeings? Maybe because no one on the *Stargazer* had been exposed to it or transformed by it, so it hadn't seemed real to him.

But Brakmaktin was real. Real enough to make a husk of everyone on the *Iktoj'ni* except Nikolas. Real enough to erase the minds of one Ubarrak crew and obliterate three others.

And until now, he hadn't seemed to have any regrets. But he had only been concealing them. He had regrets so massive even he couldn't bear the burden they imposed on him.

Not because he had murdered and maimed—the Nuyyad had no strictures against that behavior. In fact, they encouraged it. No, it wasn't what Brakmaktin had done that he regretted. It was what he had *become*.

In Nuyyad culture, a warrior had to be perfect in body as well as in spirit. Any attribute that diverged from the norm was worthy of disdain, and when it bestowed on an individual an unfair advantage in battle, it was a reason for him to be cast out.

Throughout primitive times, banishment from a Nuyyad community had inevitably resulted in death. But the banished one never protested, because he was repelled by his uniqueness every bit as much as his brethren were.

Brakmaktin was as radical a variation on the Nuyyad theme as anyone could have imagined. However, he had been so taken with his power and the rate at which it was growing that he hadn't seen himself in light of the taboo.

Until now.

"I *am* an aberration," he groaned.

Nikolas didn't argue with him. Quite the contrary. "And aberrations are cast out."

"Yes," said the Nuyyad, his silver eyes narrowing even more. "Cast out—as they should be."

Nikolas chose his words carefully. "My people have had some experience with what's happened to you. Maybe we can do something to treat your condition."

Brakmaktin tilted his head as he studied the human. "Treat . . . ? Are you saying your people can make me as I was?"

Truthfully, Nikolas didn't know if that was possible. But he didn't say that. He didn't even *think* it.

What he said was, "I think they could. But they would have to examine you first. Put you through some tests."

Nikolas was fabricating his story as he went along. But he was careful not to make it sound too pie-in-the-sky. Otherwise the Nuyyad would get suspicious.

Brakmaktin struck his chest with his fist and said, "I would do anything to be as I was. *Anything.*"

The human liked the sound of that. "We could rendezvous with a Starfleet ship. It wouldn't take more than a day if we send a message out now."

The Nuyyad regarded Nikolas, his brow deeply furrowed. "Starfleet is part of the Federation—I learned that from my captain. And we were to have waged war on the Federation."

"You're an outcast," said Nikolas. "That's our first concern. When we've addressed that, we can worry about war."

Brakmaktin's eyes screwed up. "You would help me after all I've done to you . . . and to your people?"

"That's part of our job as officers in Starfleet. We're trained to help people in need—regardless of who they are or what they've done."

The alien stared at Nikolas. "What kind of warrior helps someone who killed his comrades and stole his ship?"

"We don't consider ourselves warriors," the human explained. "At least, not first and foremost. More than anything, we're explorers. We're after knowledge."

"Knowledge is important," Brakmaktin conceded. "Many a victory is built on it."

"And not just victories," said Nikolas. "Scientific discoveries. The kind that may be able to restore you to what you were before you crossed the barrier."

"Your Federation," the alien said thoughtfully, "is very different from the Nuyyad Alliance."

"I imagine so," said the human, pleased with where this was going. "With a little luck—"

"It is weak," Brakmaktin added, "and vulnerable. I see now why my people made it a target."

Nikolas swallowed. "I wouldn't call it vulnerable, exactly . . ."

"Of course not. You are a product of it, which is why you yourself are weak."

The human felt a surge of resentment, but he didn't let it sway him from his objective. "Weak or not, we would like to help you. If you like, I can contact Starfleet right now."

The Nuyyad mulled the offer for what seemed like a long time. Then he said, "I will consider it."

Chapter Nine

PICARD LEANED BACK IN HIS CHAIR, having told his first officer about his experience on the cargo hauler. "I know it sounds strange," he concluded, "but I think Brakmaktin took Nikolas with him when he left the *Iktoj'ni*."

Ben Zoma, who was facing the captain across the width of his desk, was silent for a moment. Then he asked, "Why would he do that? What could Nikolas do for Brakmaktin that Brakmaktin couldn't do for himself?"

It was a fair question. Fortunately, Picard had already considered his answer.

"I've studied the actions of Gary Mitchell," he said. "Gone over them in great detail, in fact. And one element jumps out at me more insistently each time I consider it—the more powerful Mitchell became, the more loneliness he endured."

"Because he was so different from everyone around him . . ."

"Exactly right. So he reached out to those with whom he had even a tenuous form of identity. At first, it was Kirk, his oldest and most trusted friend. Then Kirk began to seem insignificant to him, an insect like all the others on the *Enterprise,* and Mitchell reached for Doctor Dehner instead."

Ben Zoma grunted. "Nice coincidence for him that she was in the process of becoming a superbeing herself."

The captain shook his head. "I am not convinced that it was a matter of coincidence."

His friend looked at him. "Are you saying Dehner wouldn't have been transformed if Mitchell hadn't helped her along?"

"There is no way to know," said Picard. "Not conclusively. But I would not be surprised if Dehner was like those who founded Magnia—affected by the barrier, yes, but not to the extent that she would have become a superbeing on her own."

"Except Mitchell pushed her over the edge."

"That is my theory—that he was so lonely, so miserable despite all his power, he needed the company of someone like himself. As for Brakmaktin, his urge to procreate will soon provide him with a plentitude of companions. But in the meantime . . ."

"He needs someone to hold his hand?"

"Is it that absurd, Gilaad? He may be powerful

beyond reason, but he is still a social being. And let us not forget, he is undergoing a radical transformation. It must be rather frightening to look in a mirror and see someone so imposing looking back."

Ben Zoma still looked unsatisfied. "Even if that's all true . . . why did he choose Nikolas? Out of all the fifty-nine people on that ship, why *him?*"

Picard sighed. "That is the piece of the puzzle I have yet to figure out."

It was difficult to contemplate it without considering the irony of Nikolas's condition. The very *sad* irony.

The ensign had said he was miserable on the *Stargazer* after he lost Gerda Idun—that he couldn't bear the thought of remaining on the ship without her. But if Picard's theory was correct, Nikolas's misery then was nothing compared to his misery now.

He had left what he considered to be a frying pan and been pushed by fate into the most hellish of fires. And despite Picard's determination to rescue his former crewman, he was not optimistic about his prospects of doing so.

"I do not envy Nikolas," he said out loud.

Ben Zoma didn't answer. He seemed distracted.

"Gilaad?" he prompted.

The first officer snapped back into focus. "Sorry. It's just that I keep thinking about something."

"What is it?" the captain asked.

"What if by the time we find Brakmaktin, he has already become pregnant? What if he's already carrying his brood of Nuyyad superbeings?"

The question had occurred to Picard as well. It was one thing to consider the destruction of an adult who had the power to enslave civilizations. That had to be an option, if not an especially satisfactory one.

But the idea of destroying the unborn went down with a good deal more difficulty. Even if each of those unborn would grow up to become as horrific a threat as their forebear.

Even *then*.

"Not an easy decision to make," said Ben Zoma, "is it? Of course, we could always defer to Starfleet Command."

But the captain had already opted to leave his superiors out of this. He could hardly invite their opinion about one aspect of the situation without accepting their authority over the rest of it.

Besides, turning the matter over to Command was the coward's way out. He had undertaken this mission, with all its problems and pitfalls. It was up to him to find the right path.

"No," said Picard. "Not an easy decision at all."

Nikolas was sitting on the bridge at an undamaged control console, watching helplessly as the warship approached the planet Brakmaktin had chosen as their destination, when he realized there was someone behind him.

Turning in his seat, he saw the hulking form of his nemesis. The Nuyyad didn't look as desolate as he had before. In fact, he looked very much at ease, as if a burden had been lifted from him.

Did that mean he had learned to cope with his status as an aberration? And as a result, no longer needed the help Nikolas had offered him?

Nikolas's heart sank in his chest. For a little while, he had allowed himself to hope . . .

"I have decided," Brakmaktin said, his voice again strident and free of pain, "to accept your offer. I will allow you to take me to your Federation."

The human contained his surprise. "You won't regret it," he said, keeping his voice as even as he could. He indicated the control panel at which he was sitting. "I'll need to bring us about. And to send a message to Starfleet."

Brakmaktin shook his head. "There will be time to send a message." And he turned to the viewscreen, where the image of the Ubarrak planet had been replaced by a display of sliding stars.

He's doing it, Nikolas thought, hardly able to believe his eyes. He felt a wave of relief. Another few hours and they would have been close enough to establish an orbit.

Turning back to the alien, he opened his mouth to suggest a heading. However, Brakmaktin was already beginning to fade away, turning translucent and then all but transparent and then vanishing altogether.

But Nikolas knew where he could find him—in the armory-turned-cave. It wasn't a guess. It was information the alien had planted in his mind before he departed.

Just one problem, he dared think, now that Brakmaktin was somewhere else. He was leading a superbeing of still-questionable intent into Federation space.

But he was also buying time. And if he could warn Starfleet, they might be able to defuse the threat posed by Brakmaktin—one way or another.

"So," said Picard as he reached the end of his briefing report, "we are following the trail. But we have yet to determine the end of it."

Dojjaron scowled. "Or, for that matter, confirm that it belongs to the ship Brakmaktin seized."

"Quite true," the captain conceded.

All around the table in the observation lounge, the others considered what they had heard. Ben Zoma and Wu, of course, had been apprised of the situation already. It was new information only to Serenity, Dojjaron, and Daniels.

"Assuming we find the right vessel," said Serenity, "my people should be the ones to board her."

"That will depend," Picard told her.

"On what?" she asked.

"On the situation," said the captain. "I see no point in engaging in hypotheticals."

Serenity seemed to accept that, at least for the moment. Daniels remained silent as well.

Picard turned to Dojjaron, to take note of his reaction. It was then that he realized the Nuyyad was leering at him. Not merely regarding him, but *leering*. And not just at him, but at Serenity as well.

"Is something wrong?" Picard asked.

"You have mated," said the foremost elder. He made a gesture that included Serenity as well. "The two of you. You have mated."

The captain felt the blood rushing to his face. He was about to respond when Serenity beat him to it.

"Why do you say that?" she asked Dojjaron, maintaining her composure quite admirably.

"I can see it in your postures," he said. "In the way you look at each other. It's unmistakable, even if you're not Nuyyad."

Then the captain *did* respond. "First, it would be none of your business if we had . . . mated. Second, it has no bearing on the problem at hand."

"Why did I not see it before?" Dojjaron asked. Obviously, he found the notion amusing. "Where are your offspring?"

"We have no . . ." Picard bit his lip. ". . . offspring."

"Not together," said Serenity, her voice quavering just a bit.

The captain turned to her, trying to make sense of the remark. "I beg your pardon?"

Serenity looked into his eyes. "I have a daughter. Her name is Haven. She's ten years old."

Picard's mouth went dry. After all that had transpired between the two of them . . .

The Nuyyad made a hissing noise and hit the table with his massive fist, making it shiver. "So you *have* mated!"

The captain frowned. "This discussion is not worthy of a child, much less the foremost elder of the Nuyyad."

Dojjaron's eyes screwed up beneath his brow. "How would *you* know what is worthy behavior? You are human."

Picard tried to ignore the slight. "If there is nothing else, this meeting is adjourned."

"Good idea," said Ben Zoma, pushing his chair out for emphasis.

Wu didn't hesitate to take the hint and leave the room, nor did Daniels. Dojjaron paused to leer a bit more but eventually made his exit as well, and Ben Zoma followed.

That left the captain and Serenity alone together in the observation lounge. For a moment, neither of them spoke.

Then she said, "I'm sorry."

"You do not owe me an explanation," Picard told her.

"Nonetheless," said Serenity, "I should have said something." She looked at her hands. "I was just afraid—"

"That I would think you less attractive if I knew you had borne a child?"

"Not just a child," she said, meeting his gaze again. "A young lady. They grow up quickly in Magnia."

"I have heard," the captain said, "that they grow up quickly everywhere."

"Maybe so," Serenity allowed. She looked at him. "Was I wrong to think as I did?"

A good question, he conceded. "It would not have made any difference."

"And now?" she asked.

Picard shook his head. "None. In fact, someday I would like to meet this daughter of yours."

"It's a promise," Serenity said. "Provided that we stop Brakmaktin. And that you get back to Magnia someday. In both cases, pretty long odds . . . wouldn't you say?"

He didn't know how to respond to that.

"There are those," she continued, "who would say that a man and a woman who have feelings for each other and a rather uncertain future should seize whatever opportunities they're given."

"Really," said the captain.

Her brow furrowed. "Why aren't we doing that?"

He smiled at her. "Because we place other considerations ahead of ourselves . . . and each other."

Serenity smiled back. "If you didn't, I probably wouldn't want you so badly."

He swallowed, trying to take in her beauty and resist it at the same time. "Nor I you."

Nikolas had spent the minutes following Brakmaktin's turnaround sitting quietly and watching the viewscreen, reluctant to do anything that might encourage the Nuyyad to change his mind. But hours later, all the battle cruiser's surviving instruments still told him they were heading for Federation territory and leaving the Ubarrak mining world behind.

Though Nikolas hadn't allowed himself to acknowledge it before, he was tired as hell. Sleeping on the same ship as Brakmaktin had been nerve-wracking from the beginning, and it had gotten worse the deeper they penetrated into Ubarrak space.

Now they were going in the opposite direction. For the time being, at least, the nightmare was over. In celebration, Nikolas was going to get some shut-eye.

Getting up from the console at which he had been sitting, he made his way through the obstacle course of mineral-deposit pillars and exited the bridge. Then he took a lift three decks down to the corridor where he would find his adopted quarters.

Like the armory, the bridge, and several other parts of the ship, it was growing a smooth, blue and orange skin, not to mention an army of stalactites and stalagmites. Nikolas paid no attention to them, no longer impressed by what he now thought of simply as Brakmaktin's preferred decor.

He had placed his hand on the door-opening plate and was waiting for the metal slab to slide aside when he heard something—a sharp sound like a heel hitting the deck. Though he knew it had to be something else, he turned to satisfy his curiosity.

And felt his heart start hammering.

There was someone at the end of the corridor, barely discernible in the dim light. Not Brakmaktin. Someone human-looking—a female, Nikolas told himself.

How could that be? He had believed that he and the Nuyyad were the only intelligent life left on the ship. Had one of the Ubarrak crewmen regained her faculties somehow? Or at least the ability to move around?

Then Nikolas got a better look at her face and realized it wasn't an Ubarrak after all, and found himself cursing under his breath. It was *her* again . . .

Gerda Idun.

She looked puzzled, disoriented, just like the last time Nikolas saw her, moments before Brakmaktin wished her away. And Nikolas was puzzled as well.

Why would Brakmaktin torture him again when he should have been grateful to the human for his help? Unless . . . it wasn't torture after all. Was it possible that Gerda Idun was a reward this time? The Nuyyad's way of saying thank you?

"Andreas?" said Gerda Idun, her voice sounding small and tentative in the transformed corridor.

"It's me," he assured her, and dodged mineral projections to get to her.

Before Nikolas knew it, he was holding Gerda Idun in his arms, crushing her to him. *She's real,* he thought, every bit as amazed as before, *as real as she can be.*

She looked up at him. "Is this another dream?"

"Another?" he asked.

"Yes. I dreamed this before, the other night. I was on the bridge of a ship, and you were standing there with me. You touched my hand," she said, and intertwined her fingers with his, "just like this. And then you brushed my cheek—"

He did it again, her skin soft to his touch. "Like this?"

Gerda Idun closed her eyes as if to feel it more deeply. "Yes. Like that."

Nikolas didn't want to let go of her, afraid that he would lose her again. So he stood there for a long time, holding her, clinging to a reality he didn't understand.

But he didn't *have* to understand it. He just had to embrace it, and feel it embrace him back.

Chapter Ten

PARIS HAD BEEN PRESSED into service in engineering, where Simenon was working on upgrades for their encounter with Brakmaktin, so the ensign didn't have much time to eat.

He had just gotten his food from the replicator and pulled out a chair to wolf it all down when he heard a commotion behind him—some joking remarks and then some laughter, louder than what he usually heard in the mess hall. He glanced over his shoulder to see what it was about.

What he saw was a bunch of Magnians—four of them, to be exact—and one was Stave, the character Paris had met in Jiterica's quarters. They looked sweaty, as if they had just come from a training session.

But if they were tired, they didn't show it. In fact,

they seemed chipper enough to endure a second session without any problem.

The ensign turned back to his food. The last person he wanted to see was Stave. If he hadn't shown up, things would still have been perfect between Paris and Jiterica.

Not that the two of them were at odds. They were still speaking, still seeing each other as often as before.

But the effortless give-and-take they had enjoyed wasn't that way anymore. Jiterica seemed hesitant to say or do things, as if she were wondering if Paris would approve.

What happened with Stave seemed always to be looming in the background, coloring everything that went on between them. Paris believed he knew now how Adam must have felt after the serpent showed up in the Garden.

As he thought that, he realized that someone was coming his way. And as luck would have it, it was his pal Stave.

Paris straightened, wondering what the Magnian wanted. Hadn't he done enough already?

"Ensign Paris," said Stave, smiling as he always did. "I was hoping I'd run into you."

"What can I do for you?" Paris asked.

Stave put his hand on the table and spoke confidentially in the ensign's ear. "For what it's worth," he said, "I wasn't trying to move in on your girlfriend."

Paris didn't know what to say to that. He looked around, concerned that someone might have overheard, but no one had.

Stave laughed softly. "Though it's not as if I didn't want to. There's definitely something . . . sexy about her."

The ensign's jaw clenched. Still, he didn't say anything.

"You're a lucky guy," said Stave, apparently in earnest. Then he withdrew and joined his comrades.

As Paris watched them go over to the replicator, he could hear Stave's words echoing in his ear: *"You're a lucky guy."* The ensign had thought so too.

Until a few days ago.

As Nikolas woke in the hard Ubarrak bed, he reached for Gerda Idun. But she wasn't in bed with him any longer.

With a pang of concern, he sat up—and saw her standing by the room's only observation port, wearing only her shirt. Her arms were folded across her chest, though it wasn't any colder by the port than it was elsewhere in the room.

For a while, Nikolas remained in bed, marveling at her beauty. Then he traversed the floor, came up behind her, and put his arms around her waist.

"What are you thinking about?" he asked.

Gerda Idun shrugged. "How lovely the stars are."

She sounded so childlike, he had to smile. "More so than the stars in your universe?"

"I don't know," she said. "I never really had a chance to study our stars. I was always too busy looking out for the enemy."

"The Klingons," Nikolas suggested.

"And the Cardassians."

"You know," he said, "as I recall, you were pretty dedicated to the resistance—pretty determined to get back to it. But I haven't heard you complain even once about being here."

Gerda Idun slipped her hands over his. They weren't soft, like the hands of other women he had known. They were rough with the toil of fighting an oppressor.

Nikolas remembered being surprised at the feel of her hands back on the *Stargazer.* But of course, he wasn't surprised about them anymore.

"What's the point?" she asked him. "There's no way for me to return to my universe."

There might be. Though he wanted very much for her to stay, he couldn't ask her to do so under false pretenses.

"Brakmaktin brought you here," he pointed out. "If we can find him, talk to him, we may be able to convince him to send you back—and maybe me along with you."

Nikolas could see Gerda Idun's face only as it was reflected in the observation port. But strangely, she didn't seem excited about the idea.

"I thought you wanted me to stay *here,*" she said.

"I do," he told her. "More than anything. I just want you to be aware of all your options."

She turned and looked at him askance. *"All your options . . .* you sound like Captain Picard."

He laughed. "You serve under someone, you start to pick up their expressions." He remembered a question he had asked himself more than once since Gerda

Idun's departure. "What's *your* Captain Picard like?"

"A lot like yours," she said, turning in his embrace to face the port again. "But not nearly as polite. After all, he wakes up every morning wondering if he'll survive the day."

"Just the way I pictured him," said Nikolas. He looked around the room. "I bet he would have felt right at home living here with Brakmaktin."

Gerda Idun patted his hand. "Maybe so."

"And your second officer was Mister Joseph?"

"He told you that? *Your* Pug Joseph, I mean?"

"Uh-huh. He thought it would help if he talked to me about your being gone. But it didn't. Nothing did."

Gerda Idun sighed. "I'm sorry."

"Don't be," he said, holding her a little tighter. "We're together again. That's all that matters."

He recalled the last time he had seen her on the *Stargazer*—trying to take Simenon, the ship's chief engineer, back to her universe. It had been her mission all along to kidnap him, so he could help her people develop a new kind of propulsion system that would give them an edge over their enemies.

"I hope you and your comrades did all right without Simenon," Nikolas said.

"Well enough," said Gerda Idun. "We're still fighting, still keeping the cause alive."

"Did you make any progress," he asked, "on that new propulsion technology?"

She didn't answer. She just kept gazing at the stars.

Nikolas craned his neck to look at Gerda Idun directly. "You all right?"

"I'm not sure," she said. Again, she turned in his arms. But this time, there was concern in her eyes. "I can't remember anything about that propulsion system."

He tried to understand. "You mean the technical details?"

"No. I mean *anything*. What it was supposed to do, how it was going to help us . . . it's all a blank."

Nikolas's mouth went dry. Was it possible that in bringing Gerda Idun over, Brakmaktin had damaged her mind?

It made him angry to think so. He would never have yearned for her if it meant her getting hurt. He would rather have endured the pain of being without her.

"Listen," he said, grasping at straws, "maybe you never knew that stuff in the first place."

"I had to," Gerda Idun insisted. "I was a helm officer."

Nikolas knew that. She had mentioned it to him when she was with him on the *Stargazer*.

He swallowed. Maybe it was true that she had lost something when Brakmaktin brought her there. And if she had forgotten about something as important as the propulsion system, she might have forgotten other things as well.

"Is anything else blank?" he asked.

Gerda Idun looked at him, pain etched on her face. "What kind of question is that?"

Nikolas cursed himself. *How stupid can I be?* How can someone say what she can't remember?

"Ask me questions," she told him.

Good idea, he thought. "Who are the other resistance fighters, the people who work with you on your *Stargazer* . . . starting with Captain Picard and working your way down?"

Gerda Idun shrugged. "Ben Zoma is the first officer. After him comes Joseph. Then Vigo, our weapons chief, even though he's a Pandrilite and Pandril is loosely allied with Cardassia. Scott is our engineer . . ."

So far, it sounded right. "Go on."

"Greyhorse runs sickbay pretty much by himself. Wu leads sabotage teams. Chang takes care of our small craft."

It still made sense. Maybe it was only the propulsion system that had slipped Gerda Idun's mind. Nikolas certainly hoped so.

"Navigator?" he prompted.

"A lot of people do that. Kochman, Paris, Shockey, Iulus . . ."

Nikolas felt a chill in his belly. "What did you say?"

"Iulus?"

"No, before that."

"Shockey?"

"Yes. Shockey." The woman whose corpse he had found after he woke on the *Iktoj'ni* and ran into Brakmaktin.

When he met her, just a day into their cargo run, it occurred to him that she would have made a good resistance fighter for Gerda Idun. He had even pictured Shockey in that mold, working a bridge console as the *Stargazer* battled the Cardassians.

But it seemed unlikely that Gerda Idun would have

run into her on her *Stargazer.* After all, Nikolas had met Shockey in a very different walk of life. And if he hadn't left the ship, he would never have met her at all.

He shook his head. *Too big a coincidence.*

"What is it?" Gerda Idun asked.

"I don't know," he said.

But he had his suspicions. "Tell me about your parents."

She made a face. "My parents . . . ?"

"Yes. Their names, their occupations, where they lived, that kind of thing."

Gerda Idun started to speak—and couldn't go on. As Nikolas watched, her expression turned to one of horror. "I can't remember," she moaned.

Because neither can I, he thought.

If she had told him about her parents back on the *Stargazer,* he had forgotten. He didn't know their names or their occupations or where they lived. And if he didn't know something, Gerda Idun had no way of knowing it either.

Because it wasn't Gerda Idun in his arms—not really. It was a fake, a simulacrum, a duplicate.

Brakmaktin hadn't snatched Nikolas's dream girl from another universe. Evidently, even he wasn't up to a task of such magnitude. So he had done the next best thing—he had created Gerda Idun from whole cloth, endowing her with whatever knowledge and memories he could pluck from Nikolas's brain.

Just as he had plucked the identity of the world he had meant to destroy.

"Why can't I remember?" Gerda Idun wanted to know. Her eyes were full of pain, whether she was the genuine article or not.

Nikolas felt a lump in his throat. It wasn't her fault that she was what she was, and not what he wanted her to be.

"Nothing," he said gently. "It's like I said . . . you've lost a few memories. But we can work on them. It'll be all right."

"I want to believe that," she said.

"Trust me," Nikolas told her, drawing her close to him—because in some ways she *was* Gerda Idun, and he couldn't stand to see her suffer. He stroked her soft, golden hair. "It'll be all right. . . ."

"G'day," said Tricia Cadwallader, placing her food tray on the table already surrounded by four of her friends.

"You know," said Refsland, the ship's transporter chief, "I love that Aussie accent. Have I told you that?"

"Not since late yesterday," said Cadwallader, pulling out a chair and plunking herself down in it. "And don't think I haven't missed hearing it."

"I said I liked your accent maybe fifteen minutes ago," recalled Iulus, who had started out on the *Stargazer* in security but had transferred to engineering. "Of course, I said it beneath my breath, so no one heard it."

"I didn't say it," admitted Kirby, a big, ruddy-faced ensign assigned to the science section. "But I definitely thought it. Several times, in fact."

Refsland looked at him askance. "You did not."

"I did," said Kirby. "I swear it."

"If I were still in security," said Iulus, "I'd see you in the brig for lying to an officer."

"If you were still in security," said Urajel, one of Iulus's fellow engineers, "the Ubarrak would have taken over the ship a long time ago."

"Yes," said Refsland, "and Cadwallader would be speaking Ubarrak with an Aussie accent."

Iulus winced. "Now that's something I'd rather *not* hear."

Cadwallader was glad to hear Iulus join in the fun. He had been on the away team that explored the *Ikto-j'ni,* and what he saw there had dampened his spirits for a while. But from all indications, he was back to his old self.

"You're all too kind," she said, taking them all in with a glance. "At least, I think you are."

Cadwallader had served on another ship—the *Goddard*—for a little more than a year, but she hadn't liked it as much as she liked serving on the *Stargazer.* Of course, the *Goddard* was a *Korolev*-class monster with a huge crew, and she had always felt comfortable in more intimate surroundings.

But her affinity for the *Stargazer* went beyond that. On the *Goddard,* she had felt like everyone's kid sister—one of the hazards of being a nineteen-year-old whiz kid. The worst of it was when she had to speak with Captain Muirchinko, who was going on one hundred and five. He never seemed to know whether to give her an assignment or a lollipop.

Then Cadwallader had heard about Jean-Luc Picard, the fleet's first twenty-eight-year-old captain. Some of her colleagues had expressed doubt that someone so young could do the job. She, on the other hand, had requested a transfer the same day.

And she hadn't looked back. Part of that was due to the gentle touch of her superior, Lieutenant Paxton. Part of it was due to the friends she had made.

And part of it . . . Cadwallader couldn't put her finger on it. She just wanted to be there.

Unlike the bulky behemoth sitting in the corner of the mess hall, watched from a discreet distance by Lieutenant Joseph. Foremost Elder Dojjaron had opted to eat in public instead of in his quarters, but his body language still declared unequivocally that he wanted to be left alone.

And the crew seemed happy enough to oblige him.

"Strange sort," said Refsland, "isn't he?"

Turning to him, Cadwallader saw that the transporter chief was studying Dojjaron too. "I suppose so," she said.

"Maybe he's just preoccupied," said Kirby.

"Maybe we should be preoccupied too," Urajel remarked. "After all, he's the only one here who knows what Brakmaktin is capable of."

"Not the only one," said Iulus, a shadow crossing his face. "Some of us got a sense of it on the cargo hauler."

Cadwallader was sorry Iulus had been reminded of it. She tried to think of a way to steer the conversation elsewhere. But while she was thinking, Kirby dug them in deeper.

"What about Mister Nikolas?" he asked. "What could it possibly be like for *him?*"

Refsland shook his head. "Not good."

"If Brakmaktin has actually taken him along. There's no proof of that," said Urajel.

"His name was on the crew manifest," Kirby pointed out. "And his body wasn't identified."

"That doesn't mean anything," Iulus maintained. "He could have been thrust out an airlock. Or hidden in a place where we couldn't find him."

"Or just obliterated," said Urajel.

It sounded to Cadwallader as if the others *wanted* him to be dead—as if they saw it as a better fate than what Brakmaktin might have had in mind for him. And maybe they were right.

Cadwallader hadn't met Nikolas prior to the Gerda Idun incident, so she had never seen him as anything but morose and withdrawn. But the others had. And judging by the affection they showed him, she regretted not knowing the guy better.

Of course, now it was too late. Even if Nikolas had escaped the doom that befell the *Iktoj'ni*'s crew, it didn't seem likely he would be alive to tell the tale.

"Maybe when we find Brakmaktin," Kirby proposed, "we'll find Mister Nikolas too. And—"

Iulus, who was sitting next to Kirby, put his hand on the ensign's shoulder to make him stop. And a moment later, Cadwallader saw why.

Lieutenant Obal was ambulating by their table on his way out of the mess hall. The Binderian had been a close friend of Nikolas—the closest he had on the

Stargazer—and it might have upset him to hear them talking about his pal's chances.

Only after Obal had left the mess hall did Kirby say, "And if we do find him, maybe he'll still be alive."

Unfortunately, Kirby was the only one who thought there was a chance of that.

Turning her attention to her dinner, Cadwallader reached for her customary glass of apple cider—and realized she had forgotten to get one. *Where's my head?* she wondered.

Excusing herself, she pushed her chair out and headed for the replicator. But she had barely left the table before she found Kirby at her side, empty glass in hand.

"Going for a refill?" he asked.

"Actually," Cadwallader admitted, "I forgot to order one in the first place."

She might have felt embarrassed telling that to one of the more veteran officers. However, Kirby was only a year or two older than she was. She was sure he had done some equally silly things.

A moment later, he confirmed it. "I'll race you," he said, a distinct twinkle in his eye.

"I beg your pardon?" Cadwallader returned.

"I'll race you to the replicator. Ready? Go!"

There was no time to think about it. There was only time to do it or decline—and being who she was, she chose to do it.

Of course, it wasn't a straight path to the replicator. It required her to weave among the intervening tables, of which there were six or seven.

But she had always been agile, and she believed she was in the lead—if only by a step—when she bumped into someone. It was only a glancing contact, not nearly enough to injure anybody, but still she felt compelled to stop and apologize.

It was only then that she realized the identity of her victim. Looking up into Dojjaron's shapeless face and shiny black eyes, she was prepared to find indignation there, even a little annoyance. But she wasn't expecting raw, red-faced fury.

"Filth!" he gargled.

"I didn't mean—" she began.

"I've been soiled!" the foremost elder shouted, his voice a clashing of stones.

Cadwallader didn't understand how she had soiled him, but it didn't matter. Clearly, she had managed to give offense. She would never have considered accepting Kirby's challenge if she had suspected that this might be the result.

The ensign didn't want to be responsible for some kind of incident—not when the Nuyyad was so important to the success of their mission. Lowering her head, she tried to walk away.

But Dojjaron didn't seem eager to let her off the hook. "Where do you think you're going?" he bellowed.

Sensing that any answer she gave would only make things worse, Cadwallader remained silent and kept walking. And instead of heading back to her table, she made a beeline for the exit.

Please, she thought, *let him settle down.*

But Dojjaron didn't settle down at all. "Stop where you are and face me!" he rattled.

Cadwallader was tempted to keep going despite the foremost elder's instructions. But for better or worse, she decided to do as he insisted.

Seeing her stop and face him, Dojjaron advanced on her, his mouth spread wide to expose his peglike teeth. But Cadwallader held her ground. It was too late to retreat now. Whatever the alien had in mind, she was compelled to endure it.

But before he could reach her, Kirby intervened. "Don't you touch her," he told the Nuyyad.

Dojjaron didn't even slow down.

"I said don't—" Kirby began.

Before he could get the rest out, the Nuyyad back-handed him across the face, sending him flying into a bulkhead. Then he bore down on Cadwallader, unimpeded.

She swallowed, wondering what Dojjaron would do to *her.* But she didn't want to mess things up for the captain, so she lifted her chin and braced herself.

"No, you don't!" came a voice.

Turning toward it, Cadwallader saw Lieutenant Joseph go after the Nuyyad. Though the security chief was armed, he had to that point left his weapon untouched.

Seeing Joseph's approach, the foremost elder pulled his arm back to swat the human away. But unlike Kirby, Joseph was ready for him. Ducking under the backhanded blow, he plowed his shoulder into Dojjaron's shins.

The Nuyyad swayed for a moment, arms pinwheeling, and then toppled. The deck shivered with the impact of his fall, and for a fraction of a second, Cadwallader believed that Dojjaron would no longer be a threat—to her or anyone else. Then, more quickly than she would have guessed, the Nuyyad scrambled to his feet and lowered his head.

And charged into Joseph like a maddened bull.

Dojjaron and the security officer both went hurtling into the wall. Somehow, Joseph managed to slip sideways, so that the Nuyyad took the bulk of the impact.

It didn't seem to matter—not to Dojjaron. He got up just as quickly as before and went after Joseph a second time, making a sound in his throat like grinding gears.

The security chief tried to sidestep the alien's lunge, but to no avail. Dojjaron hooked his adversary and drove him to the deck hard enough to stun him. Then he raised his clenched fist, obviously meaning to bludgeon the helpless Joseph.

Cadwallader couldn't stand and watch any longer. She went to grab the foremost elder's arm, hoping to keep him from landing a blow. But she was beaten to it by Iulus and Refsland.

Dojjaron strove against them, teeth grinding as he showered them with curses. In the meantime, a couple of other crewmen dragged Joseph out of harm's way.

Finally, the Nuyyad stopped struggling. Glowering at Iulus and Refsland, he shrugged them off.

Joseph was safe. But what had started out as a little horseplay had blossomed into a full-fledged nightmare, and Cadwallader knew she had to do something about it.

Going up to Dojjaron, who still looked angry enough to lash out at the slightest provocation, she said, "Please allow me to apologize. It was all my fault."

"That's correct," the Nuyyad spat, "it was. And culpability requires punishment."

She didn't like the sound of that. Still, she meant to endure whatever Dojjaron's customs demanded.

"What's going on here?" someone barked, her voice echoing throughout the mess hall.

Cadwallader's head turned like everyone else's, and she saw Commander Wu standing there at the entrance. A silence fell over the place, unbroken even by Dojjaron.

The second officer walked into the center of the room, regarded Cadwallader and then Dojjaron, and said calmly but firmly, "I'm waiting."

Before Cadwallader could get a word out, the Nuyyad made a sound of disgust and spat on the floor. Then he stalked off, jostling anyone in his way.

Wu watched him go, obviously less than pleased. Then she turned to Joseph, who was being helped to his feet, and said, "Are you all right, Lieutenant?"

"Fine, Commander," said the security chief, though he still appeared a little shaken up.

Next, the second officer turned to Cadwallader again. "Walk with me," she said.

Cadwallader nodded and said, "Of course, Commander," and followed Wu out of the room.

Chapter Eleven

OBAL SIGHED TO HIMSELF as he made his way to the *Stargazer*'s security section.

Iulus might have been trying to spare his feelings when he stopped Kirby from speaking of Nikolas, but he hadn't taken into account the acuity of Obal's hearing, which was far superior to that of most other species on the ship. So while the crewmen at Iulus's table believed Obal hadn't overheard any of their remarks, he had in fact heard everything.

Of course, Nikolas had become the subject of a great many conversations since the captain's discovery of his name on the *Iktoj'ni*'s crew manifest. Everyone who had known him was concerned about him and hoped to be able to help him.

Obal hadn't yet arrived on the *Stargazer* when she breached the barrier and clashed with the Nuyyad, but he had familiarized himself with the events of that time. So he knew how unlikely it was that the crew's hopes would be realized.

The Nuyyad were, after all, brutal, remorseless combatants. If Brakmaktin's powers were anywhere near as impressive as people said, he was the single most formidable individual in history—not just Federation history, but the history of the galaxy.

As Nikolas's closest friend on the ship, Obal wanted to retrieve Nikolas more than anyone. And as an admirer of Captain Picard, he wanted to have confidence in the captain's abilities.

However, he did *not* have confidence. He was frightened for his friend. And though he would do anything—sacrifice anything—to get Nikolas back, he was afraid it wouldn't be enough.

Nikolas whistled softly at the reading on the Ubarrak control panel.

Standing beside him, Gerda Idun took on a look of concern. "What is it?"

"Nothing bad," he assured her. "Just the opposite. We're making amazing time."

Her hand on his shoulder, she angled a look at the panel for herself. "That *is* amazing. If our ships could go this fast for more than minutes at a time, we would never have needed to kidnap Simenon. How does Brakmaktin do it?"

Nikolas shrugged. "How does he do *anything?*"

He didn't want to say more in case the Nuyyad was listening in on them. Brakmaktin had remained in the armory ever since Gerda Idun's appearance, making his presence felt only in the velocity the ship was maintaining.

As to how he was accomplishing it . . . it might have had something to do with their warp field geometry or the efficiency of their dilithium interface. Nikolas could probably have worked out the details if that were all he had to worry about. But he had to concentrate on the big picture, in case the Nuyyad emerged from his sanctum and threw Nikolas a curve.

"I wonder if there's a barrier in *my* universe," said Gerda Idun, her eyes losing focus for a moment.

The remark would have been cause for concern if she were truly from another frame of reference, and she could have challenged a Klingon-Cardassian alliance with a cadre of superbeings. But that wasn't going to happen.

"I don't know," Nikolas told her. "I suppose it's possible. Probable, even."

"Then maybe," said Gerda Idun, "we've got a barrier-enhanced Nuyyad as well, and he's just too far away for us to have heard of him yet. And if there is someone like that, maybe he'll find a Klingon world to his liking instead of an Ubarrak one."

Why not? Nikolas mused. He was on a ship that was maintaining a speed it had no right to maintain, sitting beside a woman who shouldn't even have existed. And their unseen companion on this voyage was the unlikeliest component of all, in that he was responsible for the other two.

So why not a Brakmaktin in that other universe?

And a bride of Brakmaktin too, since Nikolas was in a generous mood?

Of course, he still had no idea why it had been so important to the Nuyyad to reach that mining planet. But if everything panned out as the human hoped, he would let someone else figure it out.

"No response from the helm?" Gerda Idun asked.

Nikolas tried the pertinent controls—to no avail. "Not yet," he replied.

He would have felt better if Brakmaktin had unlocked the helm controls and allowed Nikolas to pilot the cruiser. But he imagined that would come in time.

And if it didn't, it didn't really matter. All they had to do was get near Federation space and send a message. And even if Brakmaktin decided to keep them silent, for some arcane reason, Starfleet would still notice an Ubarrak warship in its backyard.

The only fly in the ointment was the Federation's lack of a "cure" for what had happened to Brakmaktin. Eventually, the alien would realize he had come a long way for nothing.

What would he do at that point? Would he blow up and destroy everything in sight? There was no way to know. And before Gerda Idun's appearance in the corridor, it wouldn't have mattered to Nikolas either way.

But things had changed. Nikolas didn't want to die—and more importantly, he didn't want Gerda Idun to die. Not at the hands of a resentful Brakmaktin, and not at the hands of an understandably cautious Federation.

Gerda Idun had been returned to him, at least after a

fashion. He was thinking in terms of survival now, even lasting happiness. It would be harder to sacrifice himself for the greater good under those circumstances. A *lot* harder.

In fact, he would have been fretting about it day and night if not for this feeling he had—an intuition that somehow everything was going to be all right. It wasn't based on much—just one thing, really, and that was the expression on Brakmaktin's face the last time he was on the bridge.

The Nuyyad had seemed eager to grasp at any straw, no matter how thin or brittle, or deeply buried in a stack of uncertainty. That considered, Brakmaktin might *not* blow up when he realized the Federation couldn't help him.

He might settle for some other kind of peace. Nikolas didn't have a clue as to what it might be, but he was sure the Nuyyad would have plenty of help finding it.

"And no sign of pursuit?" Gerda Idun asked.

"Not as far as I can tell," he said.

It was curious, to say the least. Their vessel was escaping Ubarrak space unscathed, when it should have been seized or—failing that—destroyed for what they did to the squadron they had encountered. Obviously, Brakmaktin had found a way to guarantee them safe passage.

Gerda Idun moved behind him and put her arms around his neck. "So we might as well go back to our quarters."

He smiled to himself. "Don't you want to see the stars?"

She whispered in his ear, "I've seen plenty of stars in our quarters, thanks."

Then she laughed. And as beautiful as her laughter was, he couldn't help laughing with her.

Nikolas couldn't imagine what it would be like having her back on Earth with him. What would the guys in the old neighborhood say? *You've got to be kidding me, Nik. How'd she wind up with a deadbeat like you?*

It made him smile just thinking about it.

Picard felt the muscles working in his jaw as he stepped out of the turbolift and made his way to Dojjaron's quarters.

When he reached them, he placed his hand over the metal security plate beside the door. Then he waited for the Nuyyad to respond to his presence.

After a minute, the door still hadn't slid aside. And yet, Dojjaron was on the other side of it—the ship's computer had indicated as much to Picard en route. Just to make sure, he queried the computer again.

"Foremost Elder Dojjaron is in his quarters," came the reply, based on another internal sensor scan.

It didn't seem likely that it was in error. Dojjaron was the only Nuyyad on the *Stargazer.*

Given the volatile nature of the foremost elder, the captain began to grow concerned. It occurred to him that it might be wise of him to contact security.

He was about to engage the intercom system when the door finally opened for him. Moving past it, he saw Dojjaron sitting on the only chair in the room big enough to accommodate him.

"Foremost Elder," he said, resorting to the Nuyyad's title—but not as an earnest gesture of respect.

"What is it?" asked Dojjaron.

"You and I need to talk," Picard said.

"About what?" the Nuyyad demanded.

"I understand you had an altercation with several of my officers."

"That is correct," said Dojjaron. But nothing more.

"What you did was unacceptable."

"What I did was *necessary*. And if the circumstances are repeated, I will do it again."

"In what way could such actions be considered *necessary?*" the captain wondered.

Dojjaron's brow lowered over his black eyes. "Physical contact with a female, except during procreation, is taboo among the Nuyyad. Your crew member sullied me with her touch."

Physical contact? With a female? No one had mentioned such a taboo. But then, Picard hadn't thought to ask.

"I regret that you were insulted," he said. "However, I assure you, it was not intentional."

"Intent is not an issue," the alien insisted. "All that matters is that she *touched* me. An elder, no less. She must be punished to the full extent of the law."

The captain asked the question, even though he knew he wouldn't like the answer. "What did you have in mind?"

"Execution," said Dojjaron, putting a cutting edge on the word.

Picard had known he wouldn't like it. "We do not

execute members of our crew. Not even for the gravest offenses."

"Then how *will* you punish her?" the Nuyyad demanded.

"First," said the captain, "I will study the situation. Then I will make a determination as to whether I will punish Ensign Cadwallader at all."

Dojjaron's mouth twisted with disdain. "Then I may need to deal with her on my own."

Picard shook his head. "I will not permit you to engage in further violence on the *Stargazer.*"

The foremost elder glared at him. "Your crew has failed to show me the proper respect."

"They treated you as they would have treated the highest-ranking officer in our fleet."

"Then," said Dojjaron, "your highest-ranking officer should demand more of them."

The captain was on the verge of saying something he would surely have regretted. Taking a deep breath, he tried a more conciliatory approach.

"Make no mistake, Foremost Elder, your assistance is valuable to us. We will need it if we are to defuse the threat posed by Brakmaktin. However—"

"Let me make my position clear," Dojjaron rumbled. "I am not here to help you *or* your people. If I could, I would crush you all single-handedly and take your star systems for my own. The only reason I came this way was to destroy the aberration. And when that is accomplished, I will be happy to leave you to your delusion of safety—at least for the time being."

Picard absorbed the information, including the

barely veiled threat. Then he answered, in a tone that was firm but also eminently reasonable.

"Let *me* make something clear, Foremost Elder. As a Starfleet captain, it is my duty to work with you toward our common goal. But do not mistake cooperation for weakness. I am not especially proud of what I did in your galaxy. I wish it had not been necessary. But if you attempt to conquer the Federation, be advised that we will meet you with every ounce of force at our disposal. And I will be in the vanguard."

If his speech gave Dojjaron pause, the Nuyyad gave no sign of it. He just sat there, his gaze hard under the ledge of his brow.

"In the meantime," the captain continued, "I suggest you remember that you are a guest here and behave accordingly. And in return, we will do our best to keep from giving you further offense. Fair enough?"

The foremost elder didn't agree to the deal. However, he also didn't voice an objection. Picard took that as a sign of acquiescence.

"Good day," he told Dojjaron, and left the alien's quarters.

Cadwallader hung on the horizontal bar dressed only in her black pants and white, form-fitting top, her boots and her cranberry-colored tunic lying on the mat beside the apparatus.

With a grace born of hours of practice, the com officer lifted her knees to her chest and kicked out to get herself swinging. Then she swung higher and higher, until shc was exceeding the level of the bar each time.

More than once, she had been told by an enthusiastic observer that she was stronger than she looked. But it didn't take much strength to work on the horizontal bar when one was as slender and small-boned as she was.

Just stubbornness. In fact, her stubbornness might have been her best quality.

That was why it had been so hard for Cadwallader to do what she did in the mess hall—to submerge her pride and apologize to the big oaf when she knew the incident was as much his fault as hers.

And yet, it hadn't been enough. She was sure of it. There would be repercussions—and she would be the one responsible for them.

She got a lump in her throat. She had been so happy there on the *Stargazer.* Why couldn't she have lost her appetite just that once? Why couldn't she have watched where she was going?

What's done is done, Cadwallader told herself. It was one of her grandfather's favorite sayings. *No taking it back now.*

Kicking even higher, she swung forward and continued right over the bar, executing a three sixty. Then she did it again. And a third time. Finally, when she was at the apex of her swing, she leapfrogged over the bar and launched herself into the air.

Her momentum carried her forward a good five meters before she touched down. And while it wasn't the best landing she had ever made, it wasn't the worst.

It was only then that she noticed someone standing by the entrance to the gym. Turning, Cadwallader saw that it was Commander Ben Zoma, his arms folded across his chest.

"Impressive," he said.

It would have been even more so in a bigger gym. However, Cadwallader wasn't one to brag.

She just nodded. "Thank you, sir."

"I won't drag this out," said Ben Zoma. "What happened in the mess hall before . . ."

Cadwallader steeled herself for a reprimand. And it was well deserved, wasn't it? How could she have been so blind as not to notice someone the size of Dojjaron?

". . . was impressive as well," the first officer finished. "Judging by Commander Wu's report, you couldn't have comported yourself any better if you'd been a twenty-year veteran."

Cadwallader wasn't certain she had heard him correctly. "I . . . that's kind of you to say, sir."

"I just wanted you to know," said Ben Zoma, "that exemplary behavior doesn't go unnoticed around here—even in the middle of a critical mission."

The com officer smiled. "I'm glad to hear that."

Ben Zoma smiled back. "I thought you would be. Keep up the good work, Cadwallader."

"I will, sir."

The first officer regarded her a moment longer. Then he turned and started for the exit.

Cadwallader watched the door open for him and let him out. Then she dropped to the mat below her, rolled onto her back and laughed out of relief.

She was still laughing when she realized that Ben

Zoma had stuck his head back through the open doorway. Feeling a rush of blood to her face, she bolted to her feet.

"Sir?"

"By the way," the first officer said, "feel free to replicate some gym togs. The last time I worked out in my uniform, I got a rash—and I'm not sure I should say where."

Cadwallader couldn't imagine that coming from Captain Muirchinko. "Aye, sir," she said. "I'll try to remember that."

But what she would remember was Ben Zoma's kindness. Even more than before, she was glad she had decided to transfer to the *Stargazer.*

Picard was going over the Gary Mitchell logs yet again, hoping to glean some tiny but useful bit of data he had missed, when he heard the chime sound at the door of his ready room.

"Come," he said.

As soon as the door slid aside, Serenity walked in. It didn't take a former lover to see that she was not happy.

"I understand you had a discussion with Dojjaron," she said, not even bothering to sit down.

"I suppose he discussed it with you," said Picard.

"He did."

The captain smiled. "I am surprised he let you near him. After all, if you had touched him, there would have been hell to pay."

"He's a Nuyyad, Jean-Luc. Surely you've learned

that people from different worlds have different customs."

That rankled. "He went after one of my crewmen, Serenity. Should I have ignored the fact?"

"I don't think you appreciate what it took for him to come here, alone and unarmed."

Picard shrugged. "He had plenty of motivation, if Brakmaktin is the aberration Dojarron claims he is."

"But that doesn't mean it was easy for him. You have to understand how he thinks—how his species thinks. If we were the Nuyyad of another clan, we would have roasted him on a spit and fed him to our pets by now."

"So he is uncomfortable in our midst?"

"Not just uncomfortable," said Santana. "Terrified."

The captain chuckled. "I find that hard to believe."

"Terrified," Serenity repeated grimly. "It's instinctive, Jean-Luc—programmed into his genes. You don't dwell among your enemies. You get the hell away from them."

And yet Dojjaron had defied his instincts, because the stakes were high enough. That was as good a definition of courage as any, Picard supposed.

"All right," he said. "I will take his feelings into account next time I speak to him. But it would be far preferable if he did not make it necessary."

"I'll tell him," said Serenity.

Then she departed Picard's ready room as brusquely as she had entered, leaving him to his logs.

Chapter Twelve

"FOURTEEN MINUTES and five seconds," Nikolas said, glancing at the chronometer set into the upper right-hand corner of his Ubarrak control panel.

That was how long it would take them to get within com range of the nearest Federation outpost. Of course, that was only his best guess, but he had confidence that it was a good one.

Gerda Idun was sitting at one of the other bridge consoles. "I don't think I've ever seen you so excited."

He turned to her. "I thought my galaxy was going to be enslaved and I was going to have to watch, and now it's possible none of that will happen. Instead, I get to be with the love of my life. Is it any wonder I'm excited?"

She rolled her eyes. "When you put it that way . . ."

He felt uncomfortable with Gerda Idun being so far

from him—a few meters, at least. She hadn't been that far away since he found her in the corridor.

However, Brakmaktin had relinquished control of the bridge half an hour earlier, and Nikolas didn't want to make any mistakes. Hence, his concentration on the helm controls and Gerda Idun's on the communications panel.

"Tell me again about Earth," she said.

He had done so several times before, but she never seemed to tire of it. Of course, it was a subject world in the universe she thought she came from, its cities subjugated or destroyed. And he made sure never to tell her about the same place twice.

"There's a city called New Orleans," he said, "at the mouth of the Mississippi River, where it meets the Gulf of Mexico."

"I've heard of it," said Gerda Idun.

"The old part of the city is called the French Quarter. It's a neighborhood of narrow streets with jazz bars and trinket shops and some of the best restaurants in the world.

"The best of them, for my money, is a Creole kitchen called Sisko's. It's a hole in the wall, really, just starting out. The guy who owns it does all the cooking himself, so everything comes out the way he wants it.

"Man, your mouth waters as soon as you walk in. The gumbo, the jambalaya, the rémoulade . . . nobody makes a rémoulade like Sisko. And the crawfish are as sweet as sugar cane.

"But what I really remember is Sisko's baby boy—

must have been just a few months old the night I was there, and already the kid had a pair of lungs on him. I swear he drowned out the horn music from next door. It got to the point where his dad couldn't hold him and serve food at the same time, so he looked around and stuck *me* with the little guy."

Nikolas smiled to himself. "Go figure, he quieted down as soon as I cradled him in my arms. Got this look on his face too, like he was in heaven. One of my pals told me I had a knack with kids, but Sisko just laughed.

"Then I got a whiff of the kid and I realized why. It wasn't me who had quieted him down. It was a bowel movement."

Gerda Idun couldn't stop smiling. Nikolas's story hadn't been an elegant one, but he guessed it had hit the spot.

He checked the chronometer again. "Nine minutes and twelve seconds. Last chance to head back to the comforts of Ubarrak space."

"You know," Gerda Idun said, "you're a very silly man."

It was exactly what the original Gerda Idun had said back on the *Stargazer.* "Am I?"

"Without a doubt," she told him.

Nikolas basked in her presence. She wasn't the Gerda Idun he had known before, but that mattered less and less all the time. She was exactly the way Gerda Idun would have been if she had been transported to Nikolas's universe a second time.

"What are you going to say?" she asked. "When we establish a com link, I mean?"

He hadn't given it any thought. "This is Andreas Nikolas of the cargo hauler *Iktoj'ni,* seeking assistance . . . or something like that."

"But you're not *on* the cargo hauler *Iktoj'ni,*" she pointed out. "You're on an enemy warship."

"It won't be a problem," Nikolas assured her. "I'll explain before they get too suspicious."

Of course, they would scan the cruiser and find at least one human profile. But they would also find a Nuyyad lurking in the ship's armory. And what about Gerda Idun? How human had Brakmaktin made her? And if she was something else, how difficult would *that* be to explain?

You see, sir, I was held captive by an alien superbeing, but then he fell apart and made this woman for me. A starship captain might have a few problems with that.

"Six minutes and fifty seconds," Gerda Idun announced. "You'd better tell them to bring their best sensors."

"Don't worry," said Nikolas, declining to share his concerns. "I will."

He rechecked his monitors. Just about everything was working fine, despite the damage they had sustained in battling the Ubarrak. Brakmaktin had left them in good shape.

"Come to think of it," Nikolas said, "maybe I won't mention the *Iktoj'ni* after all. Maybe I'll tell them I'm an ensign assigned to the *Stargazer.*"

"That's not true," she cautioned him.

"Not anymore. But we may get better service if I let them know I was one of them."

Gerda Idun shook her head in mock disapproval. "Deception and cronyism. I'm ashamed to know you."

"I don't blame you," Nikolas said.

Five minutes and six seconds.

"On the other hand," said Gerda Idun, "who am I to talk? I lied to you about how I wound up on your *Stargazer*, and then tried to kidnap your chief engineer."

"Water under the bridge," he said.

Besides, it wasn't she who had done those things. It was the woman she had been modeled after.

"I imagine your friends on the *Stargazer* will be happy to hear from you."

"No doubt," said Nikolas.

Of course, they had no idea what he had been through. But they would, as soon as word spread about Brakmaktin.

He wished he hadn't ever left Starfleet. He could admit it now—he missed his friends pretty badly. And Obal in particular. Wouldn't *he* be surprised when he saw Gerda Idun at Nikolas's side again.

That is, if they lived long enough to see him.

Two minutes and forty-five seconds.

"Think it's worth a try?" Gerda Idun asked.

Nikolas knew exactly what she was talking about. "Why not?" Sometimes conditions allowed the network to operate at better than rated efficiency.

She worked at her console for a moment. Then they waited. But after a minute or so, there was no response.

"Too early," he said.

Gerda Idun nodded. "But it won't be much longer." She glanced at her chronometer. "Only a minute and eighteen seconds."

"And counting," he added.

"And even if your calculations are off a little," she said with an admirably deadpan expression, "it probably won't be by much."

Nikolas looked at her. "Are you saying I'm incapable of figuring out something as simple as a subspace signal decay rate?"

"I must have been thinking about someone else."

"That would explain it."

"Thirty-three seconds," said Gerda Idun.

Now he was *really* excited.

Apparently she could tell, because she didn't say anything more. She just watched the chronometer on her board as he was watching his. *Twenty-five,* he thought. *Twenty. Fifteen.*

Without Gerda Idun's comments to distract him, Nikolas was preternaturally aware of the sounds around him. The hum of the engines, louder than on any other vessel he had known—the *Iktoj'ni* included. The warbling of those consoles that still functioned as they registered minute fluctuations in engine temperature, plasma flow, shield strength, and a hundred other aspects of operations. The almost inaudible buzz of a damaged data conduit.

Ten seconds to go.

If Brakmaktin hadn't appeared to gum up the works by then, he probably wasn't going to. But he had to know they were just seconds away from contacting the

Federation. Only a fool would ignore the possibility of the alien's changing his mind.

Five seconds. Four. Three.

All right, Nikolas thought. So I'm a fool.

Two . . .

One.

It was time.

Pressing a rectangular stud on her control panel, Gerda Idun sent out a hailing signal on the most commonly used Starfleet frequency.

Come on, Nikolas thought. *Don't keep us waiting.*

A minute later, he got his wish. *"This is Admiral Mehdi at Starbase Three-Two-Five. With whom am I speaking?"*

Mehdi? Isn't he assigned to headquarters on Earth? Obviously, a few things had changed since Nikolas left the fleet.

"It's Andreas Nikolas, sir, formerly of the cargo hauler *Iktoj'ni* and the *Stargazer,* seeking assistance. Your sensors will tell you that I'm piloting an Ubarrak battle cruiser, but there aren't any Ubarrak aboard."

A pause. *"You'd better explain, Mister Nikolas."*

"An explanation," said Nikolas, "is on its way, sir."

Had he offered a verbal one, Brakmaktin might have overheard and taken umbrage with it. That's why Nikolas had put the full story in data form into a subspace packet, which the alien was more likely to just ignore.

"I'm receiving it now," said Mehdi. Another pause, longer than before. Then he spoke up again. *"Am I reading this correctly, Mister Nikolas? Are you saying there's a* Nuyyad *aboard your ship?"*

"Yes, sir," Nikolas confirmed.

"I hope he's nothing like the Nuyyad who destroyed our colony on Arias Three."

Nikolas's mouth went dry. He knew that colony. "Destroyed . . . ?"

"The monster leveled the place, erased all traces that we'd ever been there. And killed more than five hundred Federation citizens in the process."

Nikolas checked internal sensors. They told him that the armory was empty of life signs. *Brakmaktin was gone.*

And from what the admiral was saying, he had found his way to Arias III. There couldn't be *two* such Nuyyad running loose in their part of the galaxy.

But how could Brakmaktin have left the warship? And how could he have reached Arias III so quickly, when Nikolas's ship had only just made it within com range?

Nikolas didn't know. But he did know how the alien had chosen the colony as his destination. He had plucked it out of the human's mind, just as he had plucked the Ubarrak mining world.

He had allowed Nikolas to think his nightmare was over. But in fact, it had only begun.

"Andreas?" said Gerda Idun.

He turned to her, knowing that she, at least, would understand. After all, she had been with him every step of the way, and she hadn't suspected treachery either.

Idiot, Nikolas called himself. Of *course* she didn't. All Gerda Idun knew of Brakmaktin was what he had told her. All she knew of *anyone* was what he had—

He stopped in mid-thought. There was something wrong. His mind raced, trying to untangle it.

The admiral who answered his hail just *happened* to be one he had heard of—even though Mehdi was supposed to be back on Earth. And the colony that had been attacked—by coincidence, that was one Nikolas had heard of too.

And Brakmaktin had done the impossible getting there—slipping off the warship without anyone's knowing, and reaching Arias III at a speed no space-going vessel could achieve.

He was powerful, but was he *that* powerful? Or was it all an illusion, drawing on the data he had found in Nikolas's mind—starting with Mehdi's voice over the com system and continuing with Nikolas's sensor check of the armory? Certainly, Brakmaktin was capable of *that*.

Suddenly, the human heard a voice that was at once like Brakmaktin's and drastically unlike it. *"Yes, an illusion,"* it confirmed, filling the bridge with its presence. *"But where does it begin? And where does it end?"*

Nikolas didn't know what that meant. He turned to Gerda Idun, but she just shrugged.

Then he thought to glance at the navigational monitor on his console, and saw that the ship hadn't moved from the coordinates she occupied when Brakmaktin revealed his pain. They were in exactly the same place.

But how can that be? Nikolas wondered.

All the time he had spent with Gerda Idun, returning to the Federation at top speed while Brakmaktin appeared to have sequestered himself in the armory . . . was it possible it hadn't really happened? That it had all been Nikolas's imagination?

I've been played for a fool, he thought.

Just then, he caught a glimpse of something off to his left—something large and silvery that hadn't been there before, in the vicinity of the console at which Gerda Idun had been sitting. Feeling his throat constrict, Nikolas whirled to see what was going on.

What he saw made him want to scream.

The silvery thing was Brakmaktin, every visible part of his body glowing now with the light that had previously come from his eyes alone. And he was looming over Gerda Idun, dwarfing her with his bulk, *as he absorbed her body into his.*

One of her legs and her right hand had already vanished into the alien's midsection, as if into some kind of quicksand, and the rest of her was being pulled in afterward. And though she didn't seem to be in any physical pain, the terror in her eyes drove daggers into Nikolas's heart.

He cried out, though not with words. His emotions were too raw, too primitive to be expressed that way. And as he was crying out, he launched himself across the bridge.

It enabled him to catch Gerda Idun's hand as her other leg started disappearing into Brakmaktin. The pull was inexorable, irresistible. Nikolas couldn't even begin to free her.

But he tugged nonetheless, his feet skidding as they sought purchase on the deck, until Gerda Idun screamed in agony. Her shoulder was coming out of its socket, unable to bear the strain of the forces exerted on it.

But what else could Nikolas do? Just watch her get sucked in like a bug in a Venus flytrap?

"Andreas . . ." she groaned, though he couldn't tell what she was exhorting him to do.

Maybe she didn't know. Maybe for her, as for him, there was no answer to her predicament. There was only the bottomless fear and sadness that went with the realization.

Nikolas looked up at Brakmaktin, hoping he could appeal to him somehow and make him stop. But there was no mercy in the alien's eyes, no inclination toward clemency. He appeared to have evolved beyond such petty notions.

"Let her go!" Nikolas begged. "Take me, if you want—just leave her alone!"

It accomplished nothing. Gerda Idun continued to sink, up to her waist, her ribcage, her armpits.

And still Nikolas pulled, not so hard that it would hurt her but enough to slow her progress. Still, it was a losing battle. Her shoulders disappeared despite his efforts, leaving nothing but her head and the arm he was hanging on to.

"Andreas," she said again, her eyes locked on his.

But it wasn't because she wanted him to work harder. It was an expression of resignation, an acknowledgment of what she saw as inevitable.

"No," he said, his voice thick with emotion, his eyes wet with tears. "I won't let you."

But the alien claimed her throat, her chin, her

mouth. Then, agonizingly, he claimed her eyes as well, and the rest of her head. It all slipped away.

But her hand was still in his, her fingers strong and alive and callused, holding desperately on to the only vestige of life she had left. Until finally, that too began to sink into Brakmaktin, to the wrist and then beyond.

Nikolas would have held on, would have sunk in after Gerda Idun without protest, but he couldn't. To her, the alien was a permeable membrane. To him, Brakmaktin couldn't have been more solid.

So when Gerda Idun's fingertips came free of Nikolas's and slid from sight, there was nothing he could do about it. Nothing but sink to his knees and bite his lip to keep from weeping.

And Brakmaktin? He just stood there, spearing Nikolas with his eyes. He didn't gloat, didn't boast of how skillfully he had set up his little drama. But then, he didn't have to.

He had achieved his victory. He had shown Nikolas that he couldn't compete—not with a being whose power was so great it had yet to learn its limits.

Nikolas's demonstration of how badly Brakmaktin needed his company, his attempt to deceive the Nuyyad into turning himself in to the Federation . . . Brakmaktin had paid him back for those impieties a thousandfold. He had found the worst wound in Nikolas's psyche and ground a hot poker into it.

And though Gerda Idun had been Brakmaktin's creation in the first place, it didn't make his act of destruction any easier to bear. As far as Nikolas was concerned, it was still murder.

Nor was it Gerda Idun alone who had died. Something in Nikolas had died as well. It had endured the loss of one Gerda Idun, but it wasn't strong enough to endure the loss of another.

"I'll kill you," he found himself whispering to Brakmaktin. "Somehow, I'll kill you."

The alien's mouth opened as if he were laughing, but no sound came out. Then he turned away and went to stand in his usual place before the viewscreen.

"You'll see," Nikolas breathed.

"I see *this,*" said Brakmaktin, his voice surrounding the human, battering him from every direction.

And the image of Admiral Mehdi vanished from the screen. An M-class planet took its place—the same one Nikolas had seen before the Nuyyad began to deceive him.

Far from having left it behind, they were a good deal closer to it. In a few hours, it would be in Brakmaktin's grasp.

Chapter Thirteen

"YOU'VE GOT TO STOP," Nikolas told Brakmaktin, unable to stand it any longer.

He hadn't believed anything could move him after what happened to Gerda Idun. He had imagined himself immune to suffering—that of others as well as his own.

He was wrong.

Nikolas had discovered that fact shortly after Brakmaktin pulled their ship into orbit. That was when he destroyed the first disruptor emplacement in the planet's defense system, an island-based facility that looked like a high-tech octopus. Brakmaktin caused it to misfire, turning its energies back in on itself and creating an inferno of smoke and flames.

Then he had done the same thing to a second emplacement, and a third, and all the others in the hemisphere that faced him. And he had placed the images of their destruction on the viewscreen that once served the ship's Ubarrak crew, but now labored under the whip of a different master.

And it wasn't just the Ubarrak's ordnance that had been destroyed. The disruptor emplacements were all heavily manned. Nikolas could tell from the bloody carcasses that lay strewn about the perimeter of the blasts, and the suffering of those who hadn't been fortunate enough to die.

As much as he wanted to turn away, he couldn't—Brakmaktin made certain of that. He compelled Nikolas to witness the carnage whether he wanted to or not.

But the Nuyyad hadn't prevented Nikolas from speaking. "You've got to stop," he said a second time. "You can't just keep killing people."

His companion's nostrils flared. "Why not?" he asked in a voice so thunderous it was painful to listen to.

"Because it's wrong," Nikolas insisted. "Those Ubarrak were just defending themselves."

"Which," the alien rumbled, "was why they had to be eliminated." Rising from the captain's chair, he stretched his monstrous arms over his head, obviously stiff from sitting in one place. "And they will not be the last."

"What do you mean?" Nikolas demanded.

The alien's silver eyes slid in his direction. "What do you *think* I mean? I need something the Ubarrak have. They will fight to keep it until they see the futility of doing so."

"Look," Nikolas suggested, "maybe I can convince them to let you do as you please. Maybe I can make a deal."

The alien looked disdainful of the idea. "They are not deal-makers. I can tell."

Already? Nikolas wondered. Could his companion read minds that were so far away? Or was he just making an inference, based on the viciousness of the Ubarrak's response?

"It's worth a try," he said, indicating the com panel with a gesture. "What have you got to lose?"

But Brakmaktin didn't seem to be listening to the human anymore. His silver head was turning as if something else had drawn his attention.

Suddenly, the image on the viewscreen changed. It showed Nikolas yet another battle cruiser coming to the defense of the mining world, her weapons ports glowing as she sliced through the void.

Brakmaktin's mouth pulled up at the corners. *No,* thought Nikolas, having seen that expression before.

But there was nothing he could do about it. He could only watch as the warship was wracked by a series of gaudy explosions, starting at her bow and working their way aft to her nacelles. Finally Brakmaktin got to her warp core, and the cruiser shook herself apart in a paroxysm of azure fury.

Nikolas bit down on his dismay. The ship was gone, but there were still lives he could save on the surface. "Let me contact them," he begged the Nuyyad, "see if I can—"

But before he could get the words out, he realized

he wasn't on the ship anymore. And neither was Brakmaktin. They were in a sunlit plaza, surrounded by a soaring landscape of dark, spire-topped buildings. In their Byzantine splendor, the buildings had a vaguely Klingon feel to them.

The alien had transported them into an Ubarrak city—and they weren't alone. They had appeared in the midst of perhaps a hundred and fifty Ubarrak citizens, clustered in groups of four and five throughout the plaza.

Understandably shocked by the intruders' appearance, the Ubarrak began backing away from them. But they weren't backing away fast enough for Nikolas's taste.

"Run!" he shouted. "Get out of here!"

He recalled what Brakmaktin had done to his crewmates on the cargo hauler, and later to the Ubarrak on the warship. He had no reason to love these people, but he didn't want to see them die the way the others had died.

The Ubarrak were still hesitating, wary but not scared to death as they should have been. They were wide-eyed, but with curiosity as much as with fear.

"Run!" Nikolas yelled—this time twice as loud as before, stripping his throat raw with the effort.

Then he realized that the Ubarrak couldn't understand him. Nikolas wasn't wearing a Starfleet combadge, so there was nothing to translate his speech.

Still, they must have heard the urgency in his voice, and seen his expression, because they seemed to take the hint. One by one, they wheeled and began running away.

For a moment, Nikolas thought they might make it. Then he saw Brakmaktin's eyes glow with a fierce, familiar light, and he knew the Ubarrak had no chance.

Males, females, even children . . . they all uttered strangled cries and collapsed. They were dead before they hit the ground, inert bags of flesh and bone and blood.

The only ones still standing were Nikolas and Brakmaktin. Everyone else was sprawled in waves radiating away from them, looking like the victims of a massive concussion.

Nikolas didn't know how the Nuyyad had killed them, and didn't want to know. It would only make the stone of horror in his throat that much harder to swallow.

And why had Brakmaktin cut the Ubarrak down? Why had he seen fit to destroy them?

Not because they posed any threat to him—they were running away, after all. Not because they could have hurt him or stopped him or even slowed him down.

He just wanted to see them dead. And because he had the power, he had made it happen.

Just then, Nikolas heard a low hum, like a swarm of angry bees. He looked about for its source.

"Ah," said Brakmaktin, lifting his face to the flawless blue-green heavens. "It is about time."

Then Nikolas saw a speck on the horizon, between two of the buildings surrounding them. As he scrutinized it, it grew larger, and the humming grew proportionately louder.

Finally, the human saw what it was—a blunt, black vessel, not much bigger than one of the *Stargazer*'s shuttlecraft. But it maneuvered rather easily in the atmosphere, obviously having been designed to move at low altitudes.

It had a symbol on its flank—a fiery yellow eye. The city's security force, no doubt. They had come to address the disturbance in the heart of their jurisdiction.

"Go back," Nikolas whispered helplessly.

But he knew the Ubarrak in the vessel wouldn't do that. They *couldn't*. It was their job to protect the other Ubarrak. How were they to know the kind of power they were up against, or the nature of the being charged with it?

As soon as the vessel came to rest, the door in its side slid open. And one by one, the Ubarrak inside it disembarked. There were a dozen of them in all, disruptor pistols lodged in their fists.

They were dressed in stark black uniforms with gold trim, not unlike the crew of the Ubarrak warship. Their expressions were stern, business-like, not the least bit afraid. And they trained their blasters on the offworlders as if they would be only too happy to fire them.

One of the Ubarrak came forward and speared the Nuyyad with a look of indignation. "What is your purpose here?" he asked, his voice rough and impatient.

Brakmaktin didn't grace him with an answer. But as the Ubarrak waited for one, something bizarre happened. He and his fellow security officers turned their weapons away from the invader—and trained them on each other instead.

Nikolas saw what was going to happen and tried to warn the Ubarrak. But his words froze in his throat. Obviously, Brakmaktin didn't want to hear them.

In any case, it was too late for a warning to make a difference. The Ubarrak were locked into position, looking down the barrels of each other's weapons.

Their arms trembled as they tried to regain control of them. But it was useless. They couldn't break Brakmaktin's hold. They weren't strong enough.

No one was.

Nikolas launched himself at Brakmaktin, trying to stop him—but it was like hitting a wall. Though the human recoiled in pain, the Nuyyad didn't even seem to feel it.

All at once, the Ubarrak began to fire at each other. And of course, their aim was perfect, since it was actually Brakmaktin's. In a heartbeat, they were all lying dead on the ground, blackened holes oozing in their chests.

At least he can't do any more harm, Nikolas told himself. *There's no one else around to kill.* Then Brakmaktin proved him wrong.

In the blink of an eye, they were standing in a different part of the city, a different plaza. And there the Ubarrak were only beginning to hear about the alien, judging by the groups into which they had clustered.

Brakmaktin gave them firsthand experience, creating a series of blue-energy storms in their midst. The Ubarrak who were touched by them jerked like puppets and slumped to the ground, and the rest of them began to run.

Nikolas wanted desperately to do something—but what? Out of frustration, he took a swing at Brakmaktin's face. But before his blow could land, it was encased in the monster's massive, four-fingered hand.

"You don't need to do this!" Nikolas told him. "They're not security officers—just let them go!"

Brakmaktin spared him a glance, so cold and distant that the human wasn't sure his presence had registered at all. Then the Nuyyad flung him away like a rag doll.

Nikolas spun through the air, cringing at the prospect of landing. As fate would have it, he came down on a clump of corpses instead of something harder.

He didn't look at their faces. He just dragged himself to his feet—precisely as Brakmaktin unleashed another blue-energy squall among the Ubarrak who were still in sight. They fell as the others had, twitching horribly as they died.

In the wake of all that death, there was a great, sad sigh of wind—and then silence. Brakmaktin stood in the center of it, amid more than a hundred corpses, the most perfect predator nature had ever devised.

Then he looked at the ground in front of him, extended his hand palm upward, and began to dig.

Chapter Fourteen

ONCE AGAIN, Picard gathered his officers and a few of his guests around his briefing room table. Last time, they had spoken in generalities about the approach they would take when they caught up with Brak-maktin.

That was before they had followed him to the brink of Ubarrak space. Now it was time to speak in specifics.

"I have met with my acting weapons officer," said the captain, "and he believes we can strike effectively at Brakmaktin with phasers from a low orbit. The question is how vulnerable the *Stargazer* will be at that range."

Dojjaron shook his head disapprovingly. "That is not the question at all."

Picard looked at him. "Then what *is?*"

"The environment Brakmaktin creates will be a subterranean one—like the caverns in which his clan has given birth to generations of offspring."

"In other words," said Daniels, "your weapons won't be able to reach him. But we can beam down a team that can."

The captain frowned. "What if the composition of the planet's crust prevents site-to-site transport?"

"Then our team will find another way," said Serenity. "But they will get down there, I assure you."

Picard tried to think of a third option—and couldn't. *Apparently, I have little choice in the matter.*

"Very well," he told the Magnians. "We will do it your way. However, my transporter operator will have orders to beam your people up at the first sign of trouble. Is that understood?"

Daniels nodded. "It is."

The captain would have preferred to attack Brakmaktin from a distance. But if the Magnians' approach stood a better chance of success, so be it.

Nikolas thought Brakmaktin had worked quickly on the warship, but that was nothing compared to the speed at which he was working now.

Stalactites and stalagmites were building at what had to be a centimeter a second, awash with water dripping steadily from the cavern ceiling. Each deposit seemed to yearn for its opposite, lovers too long denied each other.

Nikolas could see this happening by the cavern's only real light source—Brakmaktin himself, his body aglow with an energy that had shriveled and finally disintegrated his clothing, and was probably responsible for his hair falling out. The Nuyyad stood in the center of what had been a stark, featureless vault, arms held wide, head thrown back in triumph.

At last, he could create what he had been constrained from creating before—whatever its significance. Nikolas still didn't know what the cavern meant to Brakmaktin, though it was clear it made him feel better to be in its embrace.

The only other faint spot of light in the enclosure was in one of its corners, where the sun's rays angled down along a straight, smooth-walled shaft. It was by this means that Brakmaktin and Nikolas had reached that depth in the first place.

There was no longer any possibility of the human's escaping his captor. Even if Brakmaktin forgot about him, he would never make it up the shaft.

So he sat there on the cavern floor and watched, and wondered what further horror would befall the Ubarrak of that world when the Nuyyad finished his masterpiece.

Suddenly, everything shuddered. Nikolas looked around, wondering what had happened. Then the cavern shivered again, but this time with greater force.

A milky, half-grown stalactite plummeted from above and shattered on the stone floor, not three meters from Nikolas's foot. Then there was a third vibration, as if an immense hammer was striking the planet's crust.

An earthquake? Nikolas wondered.

Brakmaktin looked up, his eyes glowing fiercely. "We are being attacked," he said, his voice immense in the confines of the cavern.

Attacked by whom? Nikolas wondered. *The Ubarrak?*

Of course. They had located the pest that had dug a hole in their world and were trying to exterminate him.

Despite the danger to himself, Nikolas wholeheartedly cheered the effort. He was happy to die if it meant Brakmaktin would die as well. That was a trade-off he could accept.

The cavern vibrated with another volley, cracking a few more fledgling cones off the ceiling. As they smashed themselves to pieces around the Nuyyad, he pointed a thick, stubby finger at the unseen source of the attack.

But before he could strike back, the cavern took its worst pounding yet. The ground shivered and cracked around them, and stalactites fell like rain.

Clearly, the Ubarrak knew the kind of power they were up against, and they were giving their countermeasure everything they had. But would it be enough?

Nikolas was still wondering when something appeared at the opposite end of the cavern. Wondering what it might be, he scrambled closer to get a better look.

What he saw was a thick, twisted piece of metal, dark gray in color. Considering the shape it was in, Nikolas could only guess at its original dimensions: a couple of meters across, maybe three in length?

He saw Brakmaktin looking at him, a cruel smile on his face. Clearly, he found the object amusing.

"What is it?" Nikolas asked.

"A section of hull," said the alien. "From one of the fighters that attacked us."

As he spoke, a second such object appeared. And then a third. And they were followed by a great many more, so many that Nikolas soon gave up counting them.

And the pounding had stopped. The cavern was still again, as peaceful as before.

Nikolas stared at the mangled hunks of metal, helplessly absorbing their significance. "You ripped those ships apart," he asked, "didn't you?"

The Nuyyad shrugged his immense shoulders. "Just enough to spill their contents into the vacuum."

"Their contents . . ." Nikolas repeated numbly. His eyes felt hot, like pent-up magma. "You mean their crews—the living, breathing beings inside them."

"They're not living *anymore*," Brakmaktin noted, as if he were talking about nothing more significant than a swarm of annoying insects.

But then, as far as he was concerned, he *was*.

"That one?" asked Picard.

"Aye, sir," said Gerda.

The captain was peering over her shoulder at the star map she had called up. It showed him a system with eighteen planets, only two of which were large enough to boast of an atmosphere.

The ion trail they were following—represented on the map as a thin yellow line—led directly to one of those two planets. Picard didn't know the Ubarrak name for it, but it was listed on the map—and in the Federation's data banks—as Epsilon Morazh III, a dilithium mining world.

Of course, there was no rock-solid proof that Epsilon Morazh III was Brakmaktin's destination. But if he meant to go elsewhere, it seemed unlikely that he would have cut through a star system, much less through the coordinates of a particular planet.

"How long?" Picard asked.

"At our current speed," said Gerda, "not quite four-teen hours."

They were only barely inside the acknowledged borders of Ubarrak space. Fourteen hours wouldn't take them that much farther. With a little luck, they would reach Epsilon Morazh III before the Ubarrak cut them off.

"Captain," said Paxton at the com station, "sensors show ships approaching. Three of them."

Picard frowned. *And* without *a little luck, they will intercept us long* before *we reach Epsilon Morazh III.*

"On-screen," he said.

As Paxton had indicated, there were three vessels, and there was no question that they were Ubarrak. They were so big and dark they looked like holes in the sea of stars.

At least, at first glance. A close examination would show each ship equipped with a half dozen wicked-looking weapons ports, any one of them capable of destroying the *Stargazer* with a well-placed energy projectile.

"Hail them," Picard told Paxton.

The communications officer set to work. A moment later, the image of the Ubarrak squadron gave way to a different image—that of an Ubarrak captain.

He was as powerful-looking as any of his people, his slitted yellow eyes set deep beneath dark ridges of thinly sheathed bone. Rather than remaining still as he considered Picard, his head moved in small, quick jerks, as if he were an animal watching for signs of an attack.

"Identify yourself," he said.

"Captain Jean-Luc Picard, captain of the Federation *Starship Stargazer.* And despite appearances, I assure you that we have come only to help you."

The Ubarrak laughed. "You've helped us, all right. You've shown us that we need to tighten our border patrols. Now drop your shields and prepare to be boarded."

"Wait," said Picard. "You're making a mistake. We've come to address a threat to you and your people."

The Ubarrak hesitated, if only for a moment. "What kind of threat?" he demanded.

Ah, thought the captain. *He has gotten word of it.* But of course, he didn't know what it was.

"There is a being on one of your worlds more powerful than anything you have ever encountered. He has likely destroyed the crew of an Ubarrak warship. We have pursued him here in the hope of keeping him from killing anyone else."

"That will not be necessary," said the Ubarrak. "An entire squadron has been dispatched to deal with him."

Damn, Picard thought. "They don't have any idea what they're up against. Send word that they're to be withdrawn immediately, before they're destroyed."

The Ubarrak sneered, though Picard didn't believe that the fellow's heart was in it. "You believe this being can stand up to twelve Ubarrak battle cruisers?"

Picard began to tell him—but before he had gotten more than a couple of words out, one of the other Ubarrak drew his captain's attention. Remarks were exchanged, too low for the human to make out. But when the Ubarrak captain turned back to his viewscreen, all the color had drained from his face.

"The squadron," he said in a voice like dry sticks rubbing together, "has been destroyed—its hulls riddled with holes and its crews drawn out through them into the void."

Picard's jaw clenched. "I am sorry."

The Ubarrak's eyes screwed up beneath his brow ledge. "If you know something about this, speak quickly."

Picard was only too happy to oblige.

Nikolas watched the pit Brakmaktin had created in the center of the cavern fill with a fiery-hot soup of molten lava.

Only the most desirable caverns on the Nuyyad homeworld boasted firepits, and none had one so broad and deep. But Brakmaktin had the power to endow *his* cavern with the best of everything.

Nikolas knew that because Brakmaktin's mind had opened to him again—just as it had on the warship, when the alien was summoning the human to the armory. And it was staying open, giving Nikolas access to Brakmaktin's thoughts.

Not all of them—just those on the surface, waiting to be acted upon. But that was enough to answer some of the questions Nikolas had been asking since he woke on the *Iktoj'ni*.

Such as why it was so important to Brakmaktin to manufacture a cavern for himself. And why he had tried to do it in even the unlikeliest of places.

He wanted to reproduce. And unless Nikolas had misunderstood, the Nuyyad could do it asexually.

Nikolas had read about the Magnians. He knew that barrier-induced talents could be passed from generation to generation. And if Brakmaktin were the only parent, his children would be as powerful as he was.

He tried to imagine a dozen Brakmaktins. *Two* dozen. So far, Nikolas hadn't seen anything stand up to the original. What could possibly stand against all those copies?

All the more reason for Brakmaktin to be stopped. But not by Nikolas. He had tried over and over again, and only succeeded in showing how ineffectual he was.

All he was good for was showing Brakmaktin around the galaxy. And how *pleased* he was to have made that contribution.

Nikolas's only question now was, how had he obtained this window on Brakmaktin's mind? The last time, it was a temporary side effect of the alien's telepathic intrusion. But Brakmaktin wasn't calling Nikolas just then. He was too busy creating a hellhole to warm his offspring.

So what was going on?

Nikolas didn't know.

Twelve and a half hours from Epsilon Morazh III, Picard sat back in his ready room chair. "Then we are in agreement?" he asked the Ubarrak captain, whose name was Alartos.

The Ubarrak scowled from the captain's monitor screen. "We are," he said.

Alartos would guarantee the *Stargazer* safe passage through enemy territory. Then he would escort the Federation vessel back the other way—assuming she survived her meeting with Brakmaktin.

Picard counted himself fortunate. Alartos was a much more open-minded individual than most Ubarrak the Federation had encountered. Nonetheless, the fellow seemed ill at ease with the deal to which he had acquiesced.

In Picard's experience, the best way to meet a problem was head on. "You look uncomfortable," he observed.

"I am," said Alartos. "We Ubarrak are accustomed to working alone, not collaborating with other species."

"I know," said Picard. "However, it is clear that you cannot handle Brakmaktin without help."

"Quite clear. Nonetheless, there are those among my people who would frown on the concessions I have made."

Picard thought of McAteer. "There are such people in every species."

"Just so there are no misunderstandings," said Alartos, "know that we will be monitoring your sensor equipment. You would do well to limit your scans to the superbeing's location."

Picard smiled. "I assure you, I did not bring my ship here to spy on you."

"However," said the Ubarrak, "you will have the opportunity to do so. Take my advice and avoid the temptation."

The captain didn't respond well to threats, even veiled ones. However, he couldn't let his ego get in the way of his mission. Not if he wanted to keep Brakmaktin's hands off his galaxy.

"I would be foolish to ignore your counsel," he told the Ubarrak.

That seemed to pacify the fellow. Without another word, he broke the com link.

Picard drew a breath and let it out. He had shared a good deal of information with Alartos. However, he had also *withheld* a good deal of information—specifically, what he knew of the barrier, the Nuyyad, and Magnia.

After all, the Ubarrak might be tempted to use the barrier to create supersoldiers. They might decide to recruit the Nuyyad as an ally in their conflict with the Federation. And they might see Magnia as a resource as well.

Alartos's people had plenty of leverage in their dealings with the Federation. Picard didn't wish to give them any more.

*   *   *

Nikolas watched Brakmaktin sleep, curled up in a raised alcove on the far side of the cavern.

Minutes earlier, the Nuyyad had walked the perimeter of the firepit, admiring his handiwork as the lava below him bubbled and spat, casting him in a feral red glare. Then, without warning, he had floated up to the alcove and lain down, and closed his eerie silver eyes.

At the time, Nikolas couldn't figure it out. Brakmaktin was capable of tearing apart starships and digging shafts in solid rock, but he still needed a nap now and then? And hadn't he said he didn't need sleep?

It didn't make sense. However, with the Nuyyad asleep, there weren't any thoughts Nikolas could capture to get an answer.

Then that changed. There were spurts of mental activity, each one briefer than the one before it. Finally, they stopped altogether, but not before Nikolas had skimmed enough from them to piece together an explanation.

If Brakmaktin looked peaceful and—strange as it sounded—vulnerable, it was because he *was*. He had entered a low-energy, low-awareness state, just like any Nuyyad who had begun the demanding process of asexual reproduction.

Back on Brakmaktin's homeworld, he would have been protected by his clan at this time because he wasn't in a position to protect himself. But he had no clan around him here, no one to watch over him while he was dormant. All he had was the height of the alcove he had created, which would represent a difficult climb—but not an impossible one.

To that point, Nikolas had been unable to hurt the Nuyyad with his pitiful human physicality. But if he tried it now, while Brakmaktin was in dreamland, with one of the stalactites shattered in the Ubarrak's attack . . .

Suddenly, the human's hands snapped together, as if drawn by an invisible force. And though he couldn't see anything binding his wrists, he couldn't pull them apart again.

"What's this?" he asked.

Brakmaktin raised his head and peered at him with eyes that were still half-closed. "Given a chance," he said in a slurred, sleepy voice, "you would kill me. So you will not be given a chance."

Nikolas made a sound of disdain. "You're afraid of me? That's the funniest thing I've ever heard."

"No," said Brakmaktin, without the least hint of irony in his voice. "You have heard funnier."

There was no lying to him, no possibility of it. After all, he knew Nikolas's thoughts as intimately as Nikolas did.

Brakmaktin put his head down again and went back to sleep. And Nikolas wondered what curses people would use to revile him after the Nuyyad's offspring overran the galaxy.

Picard considered the image displayed on his viewscreen. It was that of a green and blue world, like many in the M-class category. However, it boasted only a single large landmass, which covered perhaps a third of its surface.

There was an Ubarrak battle cruiser in orbit around the planet, but the *Stargazer*'s sensors had already determined that she was devoid of life signs. Obviously, that was the vessel in which Brakmaktin had arrived.

And Nikolas as well, if he had survived that long. As to where he was now—on the planet's surface with Brakmaktin or lying dead on the cruiser—that was still a mystery.

"Thirty thousand kilometers," Gerda reported, responding to the instructions the captain had given her earlier.

"All stop," said Picard.

"All stop," Idun confirmed.

After all, there was no telling how far Brakmaktin's power could reach. No way to know at what distance he could detect the *Stargazer* and tear her apart.

But if they hung back *too* far, they wouldn't be able to accomplish what they had come to accomplish. So they established a position and remained alert for signs of trouble.

As per the captain's agreement with Alartos, the Ubarrak vessels stopped alongside the *Stargazer*. But they wouldn't remain there forever. Even with what had happened to their sister squadron, they would move in at the first sign that Picard's plan was going awry.

And quite clearly, they would perish. But that wouldn't prevent them from doing their duty.

"Open a channel to Commander Alartos," the captain told Paxton.

"Aye, sir," said the com officer. And a few moments later: "I've got him."

Picard asked for a visual. Abruptly, Alartos's visage filled the viewscreen.

"Brakmaktin is down there," the Ubarrak confirmed. "According to security reports, he appeared yesterday in the middle of a major city, killed indiscriminately, and dug a hole half a kilometer deep. We are transmitting the coordinates."

"Thank you," said Picard.

He needed the data for Gerda to run a pinpoint scan. Otherwise, finding two sets of alien life signs an indeterminate distance below the crust of a fair-sized planet would have been too monumental a task to consider.

The captain watched his navigator work for a minute or so. Then she turned to him and announced, "Two life signs, sir. One appears to be human. The other is . . . something else."

Picard nodded. Brakmaktin . . . and Nikolas. The ensign had survived after all.

"It seems you've found him," Alartos observed.

"So it does," said Picard.

"We will be watching," said the Ubarrak, and terminated the com link.

The captain turned to Wu and said, "You have the bridge, Commander." Then he headed for the turbolift.

Now that they had tracked Brakmaktin to his lair, it was time to see what they could do about him.

Chapter Fifteen

PICARD STOOD IN Transporter Room 1, his arms folded across his chest, feeling more useless than he had ever felt in his life.

He turned to Refsland, the transporter operator on duty. "Should they not be here by now?"

Refsland checked the chronometer on his control panel. "They're not due for another couple of minutes, sir."

The captain frowned. He may have agreed to let the Magnians take the point against Brakmaktin, but he still didn't like it. He was, after all, accustomed to fighting his own battles.

Just as he thought that, the doors slid open and a half-dozen Magnians walked into the room. They were all outfitted the same way—with black boots, black togs, and the black phaser rifles that Simenon had found so impressive.

And there were six more Magnians in Transporter Room 2, and six more in Transporter Room 3. Eighteen specially trained operatives in all. They looked formidable enough to him. But then, he wasn't a being who had been radically transformed by the unimaginable energies comprising the barrier.

Picard looked up at the intercom grid hidden in the ceiling. "Idun?" he said.

"Aye, sir?" came the helm officer's response.

"Take us in—and let me know when we are in transporter range."

"Acknowledged," said Idun.

Picard turned to Refsland. "On my mark, effect transport."

"Aye, sir," said the lieutenant.

Picard had already seen Refsland rig the transporter console so that the ship's other platforms were slaved to his controls. That way, he could send all the Magnians down at the same time.

The wait was longer than Picard had expected. No doubt, Idun was exercising as much care as possible, not wanting to leave the ship open to unnecessary peril.

Finally, he heard her voice crack like a whip across the transporter room: "We're in range, sir."

The captain turned to Refsland. "Now, Lieutenant."

The transporter operator manipulated his instruments. And on the platform, the Magnians began to grow insubstantial.

Little by little, columns of yellow-white light formed about them, encasing them, supplanting them. Then they were gone. And a moment later, the columns of light faded as well.

Picard looked to Refsland. It took the lieutenant a second or two to check the results in the other transporter rooms. Then he raised his gaze to meet the captain's.

"All done, sir."

Picard nodded. "Helm," he said, "withdraw."

"Aye," said Idun over the intercom.

As she pulled the *Stargazer* back out of transporter range, Picard's thoughts were with the Magnians, who were in for the fight of their lives—and then some.

He just hoped their confidence was not misplaced.

As Brakmaktin slept, Nikolas wrestled with his invisible bonds. However, they were still too strong for him. All he managed to do was rub the skin off his wrists.

Cursing under his breath, he slumped back against the wall behind him and closed his eyes. *There's got to be a way to get Brakmaktin,* he told himself. *I've just got to think of it.*

Suddenly, Nikolas sensed that something had happened in the cavern. He didn't know what it was or how he knew, but he was certain of it—and it made him sit up and open his eyes.

That was when he saw that the place was crawling with people. Human-looking people, all of them armed with phaser rifles. And the nearest of them, a man with a red moustache, was signaling for him to be quiet.

Damned right I'll be quiet, Nikolas thought.

Then, with a jolt of fear, he realized that he shouldn't be thinking *anything.* Not when it might rouse his monstrous captor from his sleep.

The newcomers spread out, nearly surrounding Brakmaktin on three sides. Then, with a nod from the redhead, they brought their weapons up to eye level, intending to catch the monster in a crossfire so he would have nowhere to go.

Nikolas didn't know who these people were, or what gave them the confidence to face Brakmaktin, but it was contagious. The human's hopes, all but dashed by then, rose a little. He started to embrace the possibility, no matter how unlikely, that his nightmare might yet be coming to an end.

It was then that he saw Brakmaktin's eyes open.

Nikolas didn't know if the Nuyyad had caught one of his thoughts, despite his efforts to submerge them. He might simply have sensed the threat closing in around him. Whatever the reason, he woke from his slumber and glared at his enemies.

But the newcomers were ready. Before the monster could do anything, they opened fire.

Suddenly, Brakmaktin was beset by a swarm of crimson beams. They stabbed at him, battered him, illuminating the entire cavern with the savage splendor of their destructive energy.

But, sad to say, they never reached him.

Less than a meter away from their target, the beams

stopped short and splashed back. And though the newcomers kept on firing, their barrage never got any closer to Brakmaktin.

It was as if he had erected a deflector shield to ward off the invaders' fire. But deflectors were maintained by state-of-the-art machines, drawing on the power generated by the clash of matter and antimatter. Brakmaktin was creating *these* all by himself.

And a moment later, he showed Nikolas that he was capable of doing more than imitating a starship's defenses. He was capable of imitating its weaponry as well.

Because the energy bursts that leaped from his fingers weren't the nets of blue lightning that the Nuyyad had cast at the Ubarrak earlier. Somehow, as impossible as it seemed, they looked and acted like phaser blasts instead.

And they didn't miss. They skewered the invaders unerringly, without fail.

But somehow, the invaders remained standing. Was it because the beams weren't as powerful as they looked? Or because the invaders were more so?

Nikolas had no way of knowing. But as he watched, the situation changed—and for the worse. Brakmaktin's barrage started beating the invaders back. Then knocking them off their feet. Then slamming them against the walls of the cavern.

It was then, as they were pinned against the coarse surface of the rock, that the invaders began to scream.

And for good reason. They were burning up from within. But not with fire—with a pure, white energy that Nikolas could see right through their flesh.

Suddenly, he knew where the energy came from, because the explanation had been planted in his brain. The things inside the invaders were stars—tiny, unformed balls of nuclear fusion. And they were consuming their hosts with a continuous barrage of insane, subatomic fury.

The invaders should have died instantly. But instead they remained alive somehow, shuddering in an agony no living being should ever have known.

Skin and bone turned to white ash, and still the invaders kept twitching under the influence of the unholy lights inside them—their mouths open, their arms raised in a plea for mercy that went unheard. Finally, after what seemed like an eternity, they began to fall apart, to crumble.

In the end, there was nothing left of them. Nothing at all.

Brakmaktin raised his massive arms and howled like an animal, celebrating his victory over those who had wished to destroy him. And he continued to howl as he floated down from his alcove, making the cavern walls throb with the force of his jubilation.

The web of blue lightning came back and played all around him, glorifying him. As if he were himself a force of nature. *No—a god,* thought Nikolas. A savage, brutal murderer of a god.

And it wasn't just the newcomers Brakmaktin had killed, because hope had died with them.

Picard sat in the observation lounge among Serenity, Dojjaron, and several of his officers, and watched

Serenity's facial expression as she telepathically followed the exploits of her comrades on the surface. She looked alert, vigilant, like an animal guarding her young.

Clearly, she would have preferred to be part of Daniels's team, and there was no question that she would have been an asset there. She was a Magnian, after all. She had powers normal humans did not, and she knew how to use them.

However, she hadn't been trained as the others had. And her function there was not to fight. It was to coordinate between Picard and Dojjaron above and the task force below.

"What is taking so long?" asked Dojjaron, jarring the others in the room with his presumptuousness.

"Quiet," said Serenity, an edge in her voice, speaking brusquely to the Nuyyad for the first time in Picard's memory.

Suddenly she stopped speaking, and her expression changed. Her eyes lost their luster, her skin its color.

"What is it?" the captain asked.

"They're gone," she said.

Picard's jaw clenched. "Not all of them, surely?"

Serenity drew a ragged breath. "All."

There was a solemn silence as the implications of Serenity's announcement sank in. Then Picard said, in a voice as steady as he could make it, "What went wrong?"

Dojjaron rumbled a curse. "Brakmaktin's slumber was too shallow. He should never have woken so easily."

"But he did," said Simenon, "didn't he?"

Picard looked to the Nuyyad to observe his reaction to the gibe. He expected a sharp retort at the very least, if not an all-out physical assault.

But all Dojjaron did was shake his head. "He's not Nuyyad anymore. He's something different now. He's unpredictable."

"He is *still* Nuyyad," Picard insisted, "or he wouldn't have made this nest of his, or withdrawn in the first place. He is still one of your people. And somewhere in his brain or his body, there is still a weakness we can exploit."

Dojjaron made a sound of disgust deep in his throat. But he didn't hit anyone. Instead, he brought his hand up to his face and appeared to weigh what the captain had said.

"There's got to be something," Picard said.

The Nuyyad looked up at him with his dark eyes. "Maybe there is," he conceded. "But there is no guarantee that it will work."

"Tell us anyway," said Serenity, pale but still looking determined.

"It may be possible," said Dojjaron, "to extend Brakmaktin's withdrawal. To make it more like a normal span."

"How?" the captain prodded.

"The withdrawal is triggered largely by ambient temperature. By raising the temperature in the cavern, maybe we can put Brakmaktin back to sleep."

"How much do we need to raise it?" Simenon asked.

"A great deal," said Dojjaron. And he went on to say exactly how much.

It *was* a great deal. "In other words," said Picard, "until it is almost beyond the limits of human endurance."

The Nuyyad shrugged. "You would know that better than I."

The captain looked around the table. "All right. We need to raise the temperature in the cavern and we need to do it quickly. Any ideas?"

"I have one," said Kastiigan. With a deepening of the purple in his jowls, he described it to Picard. "And it shouldn't take more than a few minutes to prepare."

"Do it," said the captain.

But before the words had left his mouth, Kastiigan vanished—and he wasn't the only one. All Picard's officers were gone, and so was the table around which they were sitting. What's more, he wasn't in the *Stargazer*'s observation lounge anymore. He wasn't on the *Stargazer* at all.

He was in a cavern, standing face-to-face with the silver-eyed monster called Brakmaktin.

One moment, Ben Zoma was watching his friend Picard address Kastiigan. The next, the captain seemed to vanish.

It happened so quickly, so unexpectedly, that at first Ben Zoma thought the fault lay with his senses. Then he saw the expressions of bewilderment around the table and realized that the captain had indeed disappeared.

"Computer," he said, "locate Captain Picard."

"Captain Picard," came the reply, "cannot be located on the *Stargazer.*"

Then, right on the heels of the computer's response, came another. It was from Refsland, the transporter chief.

"Commander," he said, "the transporter in Room Two just conducted a site-to-site transport. I tried to report it to the captain, but he didn't respond. He's—"

"No longer on the ship," said Ben Zoma, finishing the thought. "I understand, Lieutenant. Just get him *back.*"

"Aye, sir," came the response.

"It's Brakmaktin," said Santana, confronting what no one else would. Her eyes were wide with pain and apprehension, even wider than when her task force was wiped out.

Dojjaron made a sound of disgust. "This is *not* going well."

Ben Zoma felt like slugging him, but it wouldn't do Picard any good. "Mister Refsland," he said, trying to contain his anxiety.

"Sir," said the transporter operator, his voice coming back over the intercom, "I can't get a lock on him. Something's blocking our sensors."

Ben Zoma could feel his heart pounding against his ribs. "Keep trying," he said.

But he knew it wouldn't be any use. Obviously, Brakmaktin wasn't content anymore waiting for his enemies to beam down to him. Now he was beaming them down himself.

"We've got to *do* something," Santana implored the first officer.

"We will," he said, pulling himself together. Because if he didn't, his friend had no chance at all.

It took Picard a moment to accept the fact that he wasn't on the *Stargazer* anymore—that he was, in fact, in Brakmaktin's cavern below the planet's surface.

And that it was the Nuyyad who had brought him down there.

"Welcome," said Brakmaktin, his voice beating against the captain's ears like a clap of thunder.

It was one thing to imagine the transformation the Nuyyad had undergone and quite another to witness it firsthand. It was not just Brakmaktin's eyes that glowed with a fierce, silver light—it was his body as well.

And it was not merely giving off illumination. It seemed to Picard that it was vibrating as well, as if it contained too much power to remain in phase with reality.

Certainly, the captain had anticipated an attack of some kind, even at as great a distance as that between Brakmaktin and the *Stargazer.* He had known that was a possibility. But to suddenly appear in Brakmaktin's presence? That was something he simply had *not* anticipated.

How did he do it? Picard wondered, needing to anchor himself in something real and concrete.

More than likely, the alien had harnessed one of the ship's transporter units. Otherwise, he would have had to coordinate all the millions of minute operations required to disassemble a living being, send his molecules streaming across a vast distance, and reassemble him on the other end.

That was impossible, even for a being as powerful as Brakmaktin. Wasn't it?

Again, Brakmaktin battered the captain merely by speaking. "It is a pleasure to meet you, Captain Picard."

"You know who I am?" Picard asked.

"I've known about you for some time. Your name was one of those I found in Nikolas's head. That was why I kept him alive so long—so he would eventually lead me to you. But fate seems to have made that unnecessary. It placed you in easy reach, giving me a chance to even the score with you."

Even the score? Picard thought. *For what?*

"For the things you did to my people," said Brakmaktin. "The terrible, inexcusable things."

Picard couldn't help thinking: *I did what I had to do.*

"Liar," the Nuyyad growled, his voice clamoring menacingly in the confines of the cavern. "You did not have to destroy our ships and our depot—and all those who operated them."

He went on to give a list of the kinsmen destroyed by the *Stargazer*—a mother's brother, a mate's sister, a relative whose relationship was so distant and convoluted that there were no words for it in Picard's lexicon. But the captain could tell from Brakmaktin's tone that these were grievous losses.

"We had no choice," Picard explained. "Your people were preparing to invade our space. They set a trap for us using the Magnians."

"It was our right to do so," Brakmaktin insisted. "It was what we have always done."

"What about *our* rights?" asked the captain.

"You have none!" the alien thundered. "You are not Nuyyad! You are weak, and weaklings must be conquered!"

Picard recoiled inside from the display. However, he didn't expect that he would get anywhere by groveling—not before someone who came from a warrior race. If he had any chance at all of surviving the encounter, it would be by earning Brakmaktin's respect.

"We showed that we are *not* weak," he said. "The Nuyyad outnumbered us, but we fought anyway, and we prevailed."

It occurred to him that the claim might anger Brakmaktin. But instead, it seemed to arouse a curiosity within him. He tilted his head as if to get a better look at the human.

"Strange," he said. "You speak like a warrior. Yet you look so frail, so soft."

In truth, it was the Nuyyad who looked soft. However, Picard refrained from pointing that out.

"Perhaps we are soft on the outside," he said. "But on the inside, we are as tough as anyone."

"Really," said Brakmaktin. "It will be interesting to see if you are as tough as you think."

Picard wondered what his captor meant by that. Then he began to get an inkling.

He could feel it in his belly—a fullness that hadn't been there before. A *liquid* sort of fullness. It was growing, pressing against the lining of his stomach, climbing into his throat—and bringing the sour taste of bile with it.

What is happening? Picard wondered.

He might have tried to ask the question of Brakmaktin, but it was no longer possible. Not when the tide inside him was rising into his mouth, filling it . . .

And it didn't stop there. It streamed out the captain's mouth and nostrils, as if he were a poolside statue at an ornate Rigelian resort. And it kept coming up, liter after liter, spewing over his lips and chin and splashing on the stone floor.

But as quickly as the water was emerging from him, it didn't relieve the agonizing pressure on his insides. That kept increasing, making him feel as if his stomach were about to burst.

And that wasn't the worst of it. Because as terrible as Picard's pain was, even more terrible was the fact that he couldn't breathe. With his mouth and nostrils full of rushing water, there was no place for the air to go in.

He was starved for oxygen, desperate for it. But he couldn't give in to the urge to inhale, because then his lungs would fill with water and he would start to cough, and that would set off a chain of torment that might kill him altogether.

So Picard stood there and endured Brakmaktin's torture for as long as he could, his mouth open, his arms wrapped about his middle. But in time, the lack of oxygen took its toll. It began to darken the edges of his vision and rob him of consciousness.

He fell to his knees, gagging, his eyes popping out—fighting the impulse to fill his deprived lungs. His only comfort was the knowledge that he wouldn't have to keep it up much longer. Soon, he would black out and lose control over his reflexes—and, bizarre as it seemed, he would *drown*.

Darkness closed around him. His face went numb, and the pain, mercifully, grew more distant.

The captain was almost gone when he came to the strange and wonderful realization that the cascade had stopped. The water wasn't flowing out of him anymore. And without thinking about it, he had already drawn his first ragged breath.

Unfortunately, it was followed by a violent, water-clearing cough, and then several more. But in time, he got it under control. Only then did he look up at Brakmaktin, who was standing before him with cold fury still burning in his eyes.

Chapter Sixteen

NIKOLAS COULD BARELY bring himself to watch the torture Picard was forced to endure. He wished he could help the captain, or at least end his torment. Unfortunately, Nikolas's efforts wouldn't amount to anything. Brakmaktin had shown him over and over again how hopeless it was to try to stop him.

Still, he meant to try. And he would have, except a thought stopped him—*Brakmaktin's* thought.

The alien hadn't sent it. It was just floating there on the surface of his consciousness, where Nikolas's link allowed him to pick it up. If it could be believed, it explained a lot.

Brakmaktin couldn't feel anymore—not pain or joy or even satisfaction. He had evolved beyond feelings, and it was driving him insane.

That's why he was torturing the captain. Not out of

hatred or a need for revenge, but because he wanted to *feel* something. And the only way he could accomplish that was by skimming the mind of someone who *could* feel.

None of which did the captain any good.

"Perhaps you believe you have proven something," the Nuyyad said. "But there is only one way for me to see for *certain* how tough you are inside."

As before, Picard could only guess what Brakmaktin meant—until his uniform vanished, and he felt a burning sensation in his forearms. Looking down at them, he saw that the skin there was splitting, pulling apart, exposing the wet, red layer of muscle underneath. It hurt worse than anything he could ever have imagined, hurt as if his arms were being slit with a hot knife.

He bellowed in pain—he couldn't help it.

But the Nuyyad was unmoved. He just stood there, glowering at the captain with his unholy silver eyes, and continued to peel his adversary as if he were a ripe fruit.

Horrified, Picard watched as his skin continued to recede, revealing more and more of what was inside— not just muscle, but blood vessels and bone. He couldn't move his hands anymore, because the skin was coming away from them too, starting at his wrists and moving toward his fingertips.

What next? the captain thought, light-headed with shock.

Then he felt his face begin to burn and he knew.

Brakmaktin had sliced open the skin from Picard's forehead down to his chin, and was starting to pull it away from bone and blood vessels.

The captain set his teeth and endured the Nuyyad's torment. But it was terrible to think he hadn't a face any longer. *At least I cannot see myself.*

But suddenly, perversely, he *could*. There was an image in his mind of the skin being stripped to the edges of his hairline and then being pulled even further, taking his scalp along with it.

The worst parts were his eyes. Deprived of the lids that shaped and protected them, they stared back at him with unrelenting intensity, piling dread on top of dread.

Help us, they seemed to say. *We cannot stand it any longer.*

The captain no longer had a mouth, so he couldn't scream. All he could do was howl like an animal.

But the torture didn't stop. Picard felt his chest turn into a blaze of agony as Brakmaktin peeled away the flesh there as well, revealing the captain's chest cavity with its rib cage and its stubbornly beating heart.

Next came his feet. Then his legs. Then his belly and his back, until his skin lay at his feet and there was nothing recognizable left of him. Just bones and blood and organs that somehow managed to keep working, though they were open to the elements and the flesh that had contained them was gone.

I am dead, Picard thought. *Or I might as well be.*

Then, just as suddenly as it had begun, the process began to reverse itself. His skin stood up and began to fold itself back onto his body, starting with his feet and his legs and gradually working its way up.

His hands were last. He used them to feel his face, to assure himself that it was back where it had been. It was. He was whole again, intact, as if he had never been dismantled in the first place. Even his clothes had been restored.

And the pain he thought would never end . . . was gone.

"You endured that well," Brakmaktin observed.

The captain believed he understood now. It wasn't enough for Brakmaktin to merely kill him. Perhaps in someone else's case that would have been enough, but not in Picard's. The monster wanted to torture him, humiliate him—reduce him to a shuddering gobbet of flesh and bone in order to exact his full measure of revenge.

"Look," Picard said, his voice echoing, "I don't blame you for being angry with me. But had our positions been reversed, you would have done the same thing."

The Nuyyad shook his head. "No. I would not have stopped at destroying the depot. I would have gone on to destroy every Nuyyad I could find, until I myself was destroyed."

"Then you understand," said the captain.

"I do," Brakmaktin told him. "I understand that you are the enemy. And the enemy must be conquered."

And he started to raise his hand.

"*Listen* to me," Picard said, remembering a tactic that had worked for a different captain against a different superbeing. "You are intent on giving birth here, in this lair you have created. But what will happen when your offspring start to grow?"

The Nuyyad looked at him, his eyes narrowing.

"They will each become as powerful as you are," Picard continued, "but without your wisdom. There is no telling the sort of damage they will do—initially only to each other, perhaps, but later on to *you* as well."

Brakmaktin thrust out his chin. "You think they will conspire against me? Try to destroy me?"

"Just as soon as the opportunity presents itself," the captain assured him.

"I agree," Brakmaktin spat, a look of amusement taking over his alien features. "They will try to topple me—and they will succeed. I would expect no less from a brood of true-bred Nuyyad."

Damn, Picard thought. What else could he say? How could he reason with a being capable of pulping him with a single thought—and reconstructing him with another?

Maybe he couldn't. *But I can push that being over the edge.* "Your children will be aberrations," he cried out, allowing a note of revulsion to crawl into his voice. "They will be outcasts and monsters, just like you."

As the echoes of his prediction died, it appeared that he had given Brakmaktin pause. And since his bones hadn't yet been turned to jelly or his heart to stone, the captain pressed on.

"Is that how you want your clan to think of you?" he demanded. "As the monstrosity who remade a galaxy in his abhorrent image?"

Brakmaktin looked stricken. He put a meaty hand over his face, hiding it from sight.

Is it possible that I got through to him? Picard wondered.

Then Brakmaktin removed his hand, and the captain could see that his adversary's eyes were glowing more brightly than ever.

"Yes," the Nuyyad hissed, filling the air in the cavern with a crackling blue fury, "that is *exactly* what I want."

Then he held out his hand, palm up, all four thick fingers outstretched—and Picard knew by the nucleus of pain growing inside him that this time his ordeal would be a fatal one.

Nikolas was getting ready to rush the Nuyyad, regardless of the outcome, when he spied a glimmer of light in a remote part of the cavern—a part that hadn't had the benefit of illumination previously. At first, he thought it was his imagination, a result of the punishment he had taken. Then he realized that his mind wasn't playing tricks after all.

It was real. And in the next moment, it grew from a glimmer into a fully formed column—one whose like Nikolas had seen a hundred times before.

It was the visual effect created by a site-to-site transport. Someone else was beaming down into the cavern—and doing it all alone, by the looks of it.

But who could be naive enough to do that, after an entire platoon had been destroyed by Brakmaktin? Who would even contemplate it?

Then the column of light faded, and Nikolas got his answer. *Of course,* he thought bitterly, as the figure in Starfleet red and black took on form and substance.

And revealed himself as Kastiigan.

Nikolas believed he understood—all too well, in fact. Kastiigan had expressed what seemed like a death wish ever since his arrival on the *Stargazer.* It made sense for him to have joined his captain in the cavern, where that wish was certain to be granted.

But if Kastiigan thought that sacrificing himself was a good idea, Nikolas definitely did *not.* He wished he had the power to send the science officer back where he came from, before Brakmaktin unleashed his wrath on Kastiigan as well.

Unfortunately, Nikolas couldn't do that. He couldn't even save himself, much less some fool of a science officer.

Brakmaktin's massive head turned toward Kastiigan, his gaze fastening on the newest sacrifice offered up to him. Leaving Picard alone for the moment, he raised his hand in the direction of the science officer.

No, thought Nikolas.

But before Brakmaktin could do anything to Kastiigan, Kastiigan did something to *him.*

He touched a device in the palm of his hand—a device Nikolas hadn't even realized was there. He wasn't sure what sort of device it was, but he knew *one* thing . . .

It was getting hot in the cavern—incredibly hot. In a second or less, the ambient temperature had shot up well past the level of human tolerance.

Unable to breathe, Nikolas used his manacled hands to tear open the collar of his jacket. That didn't give him much relief, though. The air was too hot, too thick to draw easily into his lungs.

But what was happening to Nikolas was *nothing* compared to what was happening to Brakmaktin. The Nuyyad's head began to loll as if he couldn't control it. Then, suddenly, he toppled and hit the ground. And after a second or two, it appeared he wasn't getting up.

After what Nikolas had seen him do, after all the power he had displayed, it was a shocking sight. *What's going on?* the human wondered.

But Kastiigan didn't seem surprised by Brakmaktin's reaction. He just pulled out his phaser and started firing.

And this time, the unconscious Nuyyad couldn't keep the beam from hitting him. It bludgeoned him, seared his silver skin, sent him skidding and rolling across the floor of the cavern.

Nikolas understood now. Somehow the heat had put Brakmaktin back in his dormant state, using the power of his body's own mechanisms to subdue him. But his sleep was even deeper than before, so deep he didn't know what was happening to him.

Kastiigan kept up the barrage, battering the Nuyyad, burning him, punishing him. His beam slammed Brakmaktin into a wall, pinned him there, and assaulted his cellular integrity. As powerful as the alien was, even he could take only so much of this before his body started to break down.

Nikolas couldn't believe it. He was watching something he wouldn't have dreamed possible. If Kastiigan continued his assault much longer, it might put an end to Brakmaktin.

But the bigger surprise was how the human felt about it. Despite everything Brakmaktin had done to him, to the crew of the *Iktoj'ni,* to the Ubarrak, to Captain Picard . . . Nikolas found himself feeling sorry for the alien.

Because, through his link with Brakmaktin, he could feel the Nuyyad's pain. All the things Brakmaktin had said in the armory of the Ubarrak ship—they were true after all.

He hated what he had become. He thought of himself as an aberration, a blight on the universe.

And more than anything, he wished he could die.

But Brakmaktin's Nuyyad instinct for self-preservation was too strong. It wouldn't let him succumb. And that was why, as helpless as he looked, he began defending himself.

Blue lightnings shot from him, protecting him, staving off the force of Kastiigan's phaser beam. Then some of the lightnings sought the science officer, trying to strike back at him.

The alien still wasn't awake—not completely. But he was awake enough to put up a struggle in his defense, and to gradually stagger to his feet.

Finally, one of the lightnings found Kastiigan and sent him sprawling. His phaser fell from his hand and clattered on the stone floor, finally coming up short against a budding stalagmite.

His antagonist disarmed, Brakmaktin approached

the Kandilkari, meaning to finish him off. But before Brakmaktin could reach his intended victim, he was attacked from another quarter—because Picard had gotten hold of Kastiigan's phaser.

Like his science officer, the captain blasted Brakmaktin with all the energy at his disposal. In his still-weakened state, the Nuyyad was driven backward into the ground.

But it didn't take him as long to recover as it had before. His lightnings swirled around him, shielding him, and then went for Picard as they had gone for Kastiigan.

They were more efficient this time. Within seconds, the captain was whipped off his feet and sent crashing into the surface behind him. His phaser didn't fall far from him—but before he could reach for it, Brakmaktin gestured and sent it flying into the nearby firepit.

Then he advanced on the sweat-drenched Picard, skirting the pit as he did so, lightnings playing furiously around him—still not fully in control of his senses, but more so with each passing moment.

Soon he would shrug off his malaise completely. The captain would be destroyed, and Kastiigan after him, and after that there would be no one left to stop Brakmaktin.

He and his brood would run roughshod over this world, then over the others held by the Ubarrak. Eventually, Brakmaktin would rule the entire galaxy—and he would do it for as long as he lived.

It was the worst thing that had ever happened, and

their last chance to stop it was slowly but surely slipping away. Soon it would be gone altogether.

Stopping in front of the cornered captain, the pit beside him, Brakmaktin raised his hands to unleash a storm of destruction. But for an inexplicable second, he paused.

And in that moment, the words *Destroy me* shot into Nikolas's brain.

The last time he had heard them, Brakmaktin was echoing the human's arrogance, mocking it. Or was he? Even then, the alien may have been plagued by what he had become.

But now, there was no doubt. Part of him, at least, wanted to be destroyed. And he was goading Nikolas into attempting it before his instincts moved to prevent it.

It was doubtless the last chance anyone would ever get to kill Brakmaktin, and Nikolas seized it.

First, without help from his manacled hands, he lurched to his feet. Then he launched himself into a run, reckless and headlong.

Making his way across the cavern in that dead, airless heat seemed to take Nikolas forever. The closer he got, the more light-headed he got, and the more he expected Brakmaktin to turn around and blast him.

But it didn't happen. Miraculously, Nikolas got within five steps of the monster. Four. Three. Two . . .

With his last stride, Nikolas lowered his shoulder and slammed into Brakmaktin as hard as he could.

As strong as the Nuyyad was, he could have rooted

himself to the ground and turned his flesh the hardness of rock. But when Nikolas plowed into him, he wasn't rooted at all. He was as vulnerable to attack as any other creature of flesh and blood.

So he went sprawling in the direction of the firepit. But Nikolas had hit his tormentor so hard, he couldn't stop himself from sprawling as well.

With a sense of accomplishment that far outweighed his dread, the human saw the fiery, spitting surface of the lava rush up to meet him like an immense, savage man. . . .

It was with abject horror that Picard watched Nikolas tumble over the brink of the firepit and vanish from sight.

The captain scrambled after him, hoping Nikolas had landed on a ledge where he could still be reached. But when Picard looked down into the roiling lava, there was no sign of either Nikolas or Brakmaktin. It seemed that both of them had been destroyed.

Gone, the captain thought, overcome with a dark, hollow sense of resignation. *Nikolas is gone.*

He turned back to Kastiigan to make sure that his science officer, at least, was all right. But to his dismay, Kastiigan was nowhere to be seen either.

Picard wrestled with the observation, trying desperately to come to grips with it. Where had Kastiigan gone? He wiped the sweat from his brow, wishing he could think more clearly. But the heat was too debilitating, too oppressive. . . .

Then, all of a sudden, it vanished—and the cavern

along with it—and the captain was standing on a transporter platform instead of a rough stone floor.

In the same moment, he realized what had happened to Kastiigan, because he was standing at Picard's side. With Brakmaktin no longer able to prevent their beaming out, both of them had been reeled back to the *Stargazer.*

And they weren't alone. There was a third individual alongside them on the transporter platform, lying on his back with his face twisted in pain.

"Nikolas!" the captain blurted.

"Stand aside," said Greyhorse, nudging Picard out of the way. "We've got to get him to sickbay."

The next thing the captain knew, a medical team was descending on Nikolas, maneuvering him onto an anti-grav stretcher. In a matter of seconds, he was being rushed out of the transporter room.

Picard felt a hand on his arm. He turned and saw Kastiigan grinning at him, happier than the captain had ever seen him.

"Lieutenant," said Picard, grinning back. "You are alive."

"Nonetheless," said the science officer, "I am grateful. I will never forget what you did for me."

"Nor will *I* forget what you did for *us,*" said Picard. "You displayed great courage down there."

Kastiigan waved away the notion. "It's kind of you to say so, sir. However, I am a Kandilkari. We do not prize our lives above those of our colleagues."

That might well be the understatement of the millennium. The captain was about to say so when the doors to the transporter room opened again, admitting Serenity Santana.

She stood there staring at him for a second, looking as if she were angry with him about something. Then, without warning, she pelted across the room and threw herself into his arms.

"I thought—" she began, her voice a little huskier than usual. Then she took a ragged breath and added, "Never mind what I thought. I'm just glad to see your face."

Picard smiled. "Not as glad as I am to see yours."

After all, they both knew how close he had come to never seeing anything again.

Chapter Seventeen

AS SOON AS PARIS HEARD about the Magnians, he queried the ship's computer regarding Jiterica's whereabouts. It told him that she was in her quarters.

And that's where he found her, sitting on her bed, the boots of her containment suit planted on the floor. If he had harbored any doubts as to whether she knew, he harbored them no longer.

Paris could see it in her face—a kind of awkward, open-mouthed grief. But then, it was an emotion she hadn't had occasion to express in the past.

"Are you all right?" he asked.

She didn't answer him. She just stared at the flexible gloves of her suit.

He had hoped that Jiterica wouldn't take Stave's death so hard. After all, she hadn't known him for very long. But clearly, she was struggling with it.

Paris had seen her look lonely at times, and depressed, but never like this. Never heartbroken because she had lost someone for whom she felt . . . affection.

He didn't use the word "love." She *couldn't* have loved him. *Not the way she loves me.*

Sitting down beside Jiterica, Paris asked, "Is there anything I can do?"

She remained silent. And it was a cold silence, a silence she didn't mean to share with him.

What did I say? he wondered.

Finally, Jiterica spoke. "You didn't like him."

It was true. He hadn't liked the way Stave carried himself or the look in his eye, and he had hated the liberties the fellow had taken with Jiterica.

"I didn't like the way he treated you," he said.

"You didn't like *him*," she insisted, in a tone he had never heard her use before. She looked up at him, her eyes wide and searching. "So how can you help me mourn his death?"

Paris wasn't often ruled by his emotions. But when he heard the pique in Jiterica's voice, something stiffened inside him.

"Maybe I can't," he said.

Even before Paris saw the deepening of her dismay, he knew he had made a mistake. Jiterica wanted him to be supportive, to see Stave as *she* had seen him. She wanted him to say soothing things like *He was a great guy* and *I wish I had known him better* and *I know you're going to miss him.*

And instead, he had closed himself off from her.

Come on, Paris told himself. *This isn't about you and Stave. It's about Jiterica. And if you feel about her the way you say, you'll put your jealousy aside and help her get past this.*

"No," he said, "that's wrong. I *can* help. I . . ."

The ensign wanted to say the right things. He really did. He just couldn't bring himself to do it.

"Yes?" said Jiterica.

Stave was dead. Whatever jealousy or resentment Paris had felt should have ended with the Magnian's demise.

Should have. But when he looked at Jiterica and saw how badly Stave's death was affecting her, he couldn't help feeling jealous and resentful all over again.

After a while, she turned away from him. And he knew that this time, she wasn't turning back.

"Sorry," Paris mumbled.

Jiterica didn't answer him.

It was clear that she didn't want him there, so he told her he would see her later and left her quarters the way he had come in. As her door whispered closed behind him, Paris felt terrible.

He had let Jiterica down when she needed him. He had failed her. And he wasn't sure she would ever forget it.

Stave was dead, unable to compete anymore for Jiterica's affection. And yet somehow, even in absentia, he had won.

Captain's Log, Supplemental. Nikolas was badly burned from his proximity to the lava. However, thanks to the skill of Doctor Greyhorse, Nikolas will not only survive, but will hardly have a scar to show for his ordeal.

Picard looked down at Nikolas, who was still asleep on a biobed in Greyhorse's sickbay. The entire left side of the man's face looked red and raw. But then, the skin there was newly regenerated, and therefore still tender.

The captain tried to imagine what had gone through Nikolas's mind as he charged Brakmaktin. No doubt, he had seen terrible things in the Nuyyad's company, the deaths of his crewmates on the *Iktoj'ni* not the least of them. But to sacrifice his life so readily, with such determination . . .

"Captain," said a familiar voice.

Picard turned to Greyhorse, who had emerged from his office. "Shouldn't we be quiet so your patient can rest?"

"He's rested enough for one morning," said the doctor. "It's time for him to rejoin the ranks of the living."

Reaching into the pocket of his lab coat, he fished out a hypospray. Adjusting the formulation, he applied the device to Nikolas's neck and released the contents.

Nothing happened at first. Then the patient's eyelids began to flutter and he looked around.

For a moment, the look in his eyes was vacant, hollow. It was as if he were still bearing witness to an unnameable horror. Then his eyes focused on the captain's face.

"Sir," he said, making an attempt to sit up.

Picard gently pressed him back down again. "Don't," he said, "or the doctor will eject me from sickbay."

Nikolas frowned a little, limited by the constraints of his new skin. "I don't doubt it."

"How are you feeling?" Picard asked.

"A lot better, sir."

And yet, Picard thought, *you still bear the scars of what you experienced—not on your face, perhaps, but elsewhere.*

But what he said was, "You certainly *look* better. I am pleased to see you are making such exemplary progress."

Nikolas gave Greyhorse a sidelong glance. "Thanks to the doctor."

Picard glanced at Greyhorse too. "Yes, it is always good to acknowledge the efforts of one's physician, especially when one has yet to leave sickbay."

"Flattery," said the doctor, "will avail you nothing."

The captain smiled, but Nikolas did not. Either he was prevented from it by his injuries or he simply couldn't find it in himself—it was difficult to say which.

"You know," said Picard, "Lieutenant Obal's been here every chance he gets. He must be a good friend."

"The best," Nikolas said, his eyes brightening a little at the mention of the Binderian.

"I need not tell you how pleased he was to see you again. But then we all were, myself included."

Nikolas's brow furrowed as much as it could under the circumstances. "I don't suppose . . ."

Picard looked at him. "What?"

The younger man swallowed. "If it's all right with you, sir, I'd like to come back to the *Stargazer.*"

"Back?" asked the captain, surprised by the request.

"As a member of the crew, sir. I know I sort of burned that bridge behind me, but I thought . . ." His voice trailed off hopefully.

Picard considered the possibility for a moment. "It is not as if I have taken on anyone new in your place. And it would be a good deal more convenient for all concerned if we did not have to train someone from scratch."

Nikolas almost looked happy. "Then . . . ?"

"Welcome home," said Picard. "Just do me a favor and stay awhile this time. Yes?"

Nikolas nodded. "Absolutely, sir."

The captain patted him on the shoulder. Then, with a nod to Greyhorse, he left sickbay.

Imagine that, he thought. *I have my ensign back.*

Picard was pleased to have had the opportunity to give Nikolas his old job. He just didn't know how long he would be privileged to keep his own.

Nol Kastiigan had considered ordering a hot dish from the replicator in the *Stargazer*'s mess hall. However, he decided to get something cold instead.

He had had enough heat to last him quite some time.

After a moment's deliberation, Kastiigan settled on a marinated Mediterranean seafood platter to which Commander Ben Zoma had introduced him a few weeks earlier. He was already enjoying the tangy, sea-salty scent of it as he crossed the room and looked for a place to sit.

"Hey, Lieutenant!" someone called.

Looking around, Kastiigan saw Lieutenant Refsland beckoning to him. He was sitting with Iulus and Kochman, both of whom appeared eager for the science officer's company.

Smiling to himself, Kastiigan joined them. "How are all of you this morning?" he asked.

"The question," said Kochman, "is, how are *you?*"

"Any ill effects from that heat bomb?" asked Refsland.

"None," Kastiigan was pleased to say.

They all agreed that that was good. They didn't want him to experience any discomfort, considering he had saved the *Stargazer,* an Ubarrak world, and possibly the entire galaxy.

"Don't worry," he assured them. "I'm fine."

He was about to dig into his seafood dish when he heard someone else call his name. Looking up, he saw that a number of other colleagues had gathered around him.

"You're the man," said Dubinksi, one of Simenon's engineers.

"We're proud of you," added Cadwallader.

"Thank you," he told them.

The science officer had become rather popular since his foray into Brakmaktin's cavern. Everyone on the *Stargazer* seemed to have heard about it.

And everyone at Starfleet Command would hear of it too, if they hadn't already. In Captain Picard's report, he had recommended Kastiigan for a medal of valor.

If it was approved, it would be the first such honor accorded to a Kandilkari. His family would be happy to receive the news—especially his grandfather, who had encouraged him to join Starfleet in the first place.

"Lieutenant?" someone said.

Kastiigan turned again and saw that it was Nikolas standing beside him. And the ensign had healed, a small pink scar on his cheek the only remaining evidence of the terrible ordeal Brakmaktin had put him through.

"Yes?" said the science officer.

"I just wanted to say . . . well, good going down there. If not for you, I'd still be Brakmaktin's whipping boy."

Kastiigan smiled yet again. "You're quite welcome."

"If you ever need a hand," said Nikolas, "just say the word, all right?"

The Kandilkari nodded. "I will do that."

Nikolas clapped him on the shoulder, despite the difference in their ranks. Then he went to join his friend Obal on the replicator line.

Naturally, Kastiigan took pleasure from the accolades of his comrades. Anyone would have.

However, his biggest satisfaction came from the knowledge that he had finally done what he joined Starfleet to do—he had risked his life against a formidable enemy, in a situation where the odds seemed stacked against him.

As it happened, Kastiigan had survived the confrontation. But that was hardly his fault. The important thing was that he *could* have lost his life.

Besides, there would be other opportunities for him to show what he was made of. It was only a matter of time before one of them claimed his life, he thought optimistically, and took another forkful of his dinner.

Picard was just returning to the bridge when he heard Gerda's voice ring from bulkhead to bulkhead.

"Commander," she said, "the Ubarrak are breaking formation."

Wu, who was ensconced in the center seat, got up and took a step toward the viewscreen—where Alartos's warships were taking positions in close proximity to the *Stargazer.*

If the Ubarrak wished, they could catch the Federation vessel in a devastating crossfire. Picard and his crew wouldn't stand a chance.

Wu took note of the captain's presence. "Treachery?"

From what he had seen of Alartos, he didn't think so.

"Shall I power weapons?" asked Gerda, her voice husky with the urge to do battle.

Trusting his instincts, Picard shook his head. "No."

Then Paxton relieved the tension somewhat. "They're hailing us," he reported.

Picard eyed the viewscreen. "Respond."

A moment later, Alartos's face appeared. He looked as imperious as when the captain had first seen him.

"We have reached the limits of Ubarrak space," he said. "You may continue from this point on your own."

"Thank you," said Picard.

They were well past the border accepted by the Federation. However, the captain didn't think this was the time or place to make that point.

"I hope you know," said Alartos, thrusting his chin out in a typically Ubarrak gesture of belligerence, "you haven't won any favors from my people."

Picard smiled. "I never expected any."

As he had learned years earlier, the Ubarrak didn't even have a *word* for gratitude. And if they had, Alartos wouldn't have used it on a human—someone whose species was at odds with his own.

But the captain knew what he had done for Alartos's people. He had saved them from a grotesque and terrifying fate, maybe even annihilation, and that was thanks enough for him.

The Ubarrak nodded, apparently satisfied with Picard's response. "Good," he rasped.

But there was something in his eyes that belied his last statement, something that told the human that he had indeed won something—a measure of respect, perhaps, if not from the Ubarrak in general, then at least from Alartos himself.

Then the commander's image vanished from Picard's viewscreen, to be replaced by that of his trio of ships. The message was crystal-clear: the *Stargazer*'s business here was finished. It was time to leave.

The captain glanced playfully at Idun. "Feisty," he observed, "aren't they?"

The helm officer returned only a hint of a smile. "They would not last ten minutes on Qo'noS."

Picard wasn't so certain about that, but he wasn't inclined to disagree out loud. He would have plenty of chances to do that when he faced his tribunal.

And thanks to the choices he had made of late, McAteer had even more ammunition than before.

"Earth," he told Idun. "Best speed."

Chapter Eighteen

PICARD SAT ON A CHAIR in his quarters, alone.

He could have continued to have Serenity's company, as he had whenever possible the last few days, and a part of him longed for it as much as ever. However, another part needed time to think, a chance to put matters into some kind of perspective.

Serenity had been kind enough to understand how he felt. And so had Ben Zoma, when he offered to stand vigil with his friend and Picard had gently declined.

A captain, after all, was ultimately an island, the poet John Donne notwithstanding. And Picard preferred to face his last hours as commanding officer of the *Stargazer* on his own.

He wasn't going down with his ship, like the captains of old. As it happened, he was going down *with-*

out it. But either way, it was time he came to grips with his prospects.

McAteer wouldn't have called for a hearing if he didn't think he could obtain the verdict he wanted. And with Admiral Caber sitting on the jury, Picard's fate was sealed.

When he returned to the ship afterward, it wouldn't be to give orders. It would be to clean out his quarters so his successor could move in. Someone more to McAteer's liking, presumably.

So this would be his only time to measure his brief but eventful time in the center seat. To understand its place in his life. And of course, to say good-bye, at least in his mind.

It was a good crew Picard had commanded, a courageous crew that had done well under the most adverse of circumstances. He expected that they would do great things, together and individually, and that he would be proud of them in times to come.

As for the *Stargazer* . . . there was a reason ships had always been referred to as females. He would miss her as much as he missed any flesh-and-blood comrade, from the engines that had carried him so faithfully through the void to the proud plaque on her bridge—the one that said "To bring light into the darkness."

Perhaps, the captain thought, *we brought a little light, if not quite as much as I intended.*

In any case, the *Stargazer* would go on. And so would her crew. Ships and crews always did.

But what about me?

It wasn't a question Picard would have asked of anyone else—not even those closest to him, for fear of sounding self-indulgent. But here, in the privacy of his solitude, he could ask it.

For as long as he could remember, he had dreamed of captaining a starship. That had been his life. Of course, he hadn't expected to have a command handed to him at the age of twenty-eight, but he had hoped he would receive one eventually.

And now that command would be taken away. What was a man supposed to do when his dreams were stripped from him? The captain didn't know. But when his tribunal ruled against him, he would be compelled to find out.

Just then, he heard his door chime, announcing a caller. Not Serenity or Ben Zoma, certainly. Then who?

"Come," he said.

When the doors slid open, they revealed Pug Joseph. The security chief seemed to hesitate for a moment before entering the room, as if he didn't feel quite comfortable being there.

"Lieutenant," said Picard, wondering what was wrong. "What can I do for you?"

The lieutenant shrugged. "Actually," he said, "there's something I'd like to do for you, sir."

"Oh?" said the captain. He sat back in his chair. "And what might that be?"

Joseph opened his hand and held it out to Picard, showing him a glass sphere about the size of a man's fingernail. The light seemed to melt in its amber depths.

Picard looked at his visitor. "A marble?"

The security officer blushed. "Yes, sir. You see, it was my lucky charm when I was little, and it got me through some tough scrapes. So I brought it with me into space, and I carry it sometimes. I mean, on away missions and such."

The captain smiled. "Are you . . . offering it to me?"

Joseph nodded. "I figure you're going to need some kind of luck when we get back to Earth. In that . . ." He shrugged.

"Hearing," Picard suggested.

"Yes. That hearing. I know it's kind of stupid, but—"

Picard stopped him with a raised hand. "No," he said, touched by the gesture. "It is not stupid at all."

He took the marble and rolled it between his fingers, examining the buttery swirls of color trapped within it. It didn't seem possible that it would stop Admiral McAteer.

But then, he reminded himself, it hadn't seemed possible that anyone would stop Brakmaktin either.

Picard looked to the lieutenant again. "Who knows? Perhaps it will do for me what it has done for you." And he slipped it into an inner pocket of his jacket.

Joseph nodded approvingly. "I hope so, sir."

The captain sighed. *So do I.*

Picard reported early to the small, windowless courtroom where his case was scheduled to be heard, and took the seat that had been reserved for him.

It was one of only four in the front of the room. The

other three, set aside for the admirals who would judge the captain and his record, faced him from behind a long table.

There were seats in the back of the room as well— an even dozen of them, arranged in two rows on either side of a central aisle. They would accommodate whatever spectators cared to attend the hearing, since—by agreement of all parties concerned—it was to be an open proceeding.

Picard sat back in his chair and closed his eyes. *Finally,* he thought, *it has come to this.* He had been thinking about it for weeks, preparing himself for it, but the reality was weightier than anything he had imagined.

If the jury of three ruled against him, he would lose his command. It was that simple.

It would be difficult to turn his ship and crew over to someone else. *A little like turning one's children over to another father.* But he would have no choice in the matter, and no possibility of appeal. In accordance with Starfleet regulations, the admirals' decision would be final.

For several minutes, he continued to sit there by himself, girding himself for the inevitable. Then he heard the door slide open and looked back over his shoulder.

It was McAteer, dress uniform and all. He spared the captain a look of sympathy as he moved by him, as if he were sorry all this had to take place.

Of course you are, Picard thought.

There was a minute or two when he and McAteer

were the only people in the room. It was not a comfort-able stretch of time—for either of them, the captain imagined.

Then the door opened again and Admiral Mehdi walked in. He looked vaguely dissatisfied, as was his custom. Normally, Picard wondered why the man didn't look happier, but on this occasion he knew all too well.

Finally, Caber entered the room. He was a tall, strapping man with dark hair, not unlike his son. But his face was narrower and sterner, and a goatee covered the lower half of it.

He didn't look at Picard, but he had to know who the captain was and what he had done to the younger Caber. It had to be in the back of his mind, coloring whatever ruling he made.

And that, even more than McAteer's active disdain, was what gave Picard cause for concern.

Only when the judges were seated did the security guards at the door permit the gallery to file in. Picard didn't look back to see their faces, but he was certain that Ben Zoma would be among them, and perhaps some of his other officers as well.

When everyone was seated, McAteer stood and addressed the room. "This hearing is hereby con-vened," he said, "its purpose to review the actions of Jean-Luc Picard, captain of the *U.S.S. Stargazer,* and decide whether he is qualified to go forward as a com-manding officer in Starfleet."

He turned to Picard. "Captain, do you have any questions before we proceed?"

"None, sir," said Picard.

McAteer came around the table at which his colleagues were sitting and took up a spot at the captain's right hand, from which position he could address both Picard and his fellow admirals. Then he paused for a moment, apparently to gather his thoughts.

"Captain," he said at last, "several months ago, on the far side of the galactic barrier, you encountered a species known as the Nuyyad. Is this correct?"

"It is," said Picard.

"And in a first-contact situation with the Nuyyad, you fired your weapons at their vessels without first attempting to communicate with them. Is this also true?"

"My predecessor, Captain Ruhalter, made that attempt," said Picard. "The Nuyyad ignored it and attacked us. It was Captain Ruhalter who fired back initially, having been left little choice in the matter."

"Little choice?" McAteer echoed, putting an ironic spin on the phrase. "The *Stargazer* was in unfamiliar space, which may well have belonged to the Nuyyad. Why didn't Captain Ruhalter simply withdraw from the encounter?"

"He did," said Picard.

"But," the admiral pressed, "only after he had already exchanged volleys with the Nuyyad."

Picard nodded. "That is correct."

"Nonetheless, the battle was rejoined, and both Captain Ruhalter and Commander Leach—your first officer—were rendered incapable of command. That left you the highest-ranking officer aboard. At that juncture, you could have made your own attempt to communicate with the Nuyyad. However, you rejected that option in favor of continued hostilities. True?"

"The *Stargazer* was under attack," said Picard. "My immediate superiors were already dead or incapacitated. It was imperative that I extricate my ship from danger."

"Which you accomplished," McAteer noted, "by destroying the Nuyyad's ship."

It was ironic. The last time he heard that charge, it had come from Brakmaktin. And all he could tell the admiral was what he had told the Nuyyad.

"They were pursuing us," the captain explained. "It was either destroy them or *be* destroyed."

"How do you know that if you neglected to contact them?"

Picard frowned. "It was clear to me that they were not interested in a peaceful resolution—not only because they had failed to respond to Captain Ruhalter's hails, but because of the tenacity of their pursuit and the level of firepower they brought to bear."

"But," said McAteer, "for the record . . . you chose to destroy them rather than make another attempt at communication."

The captain's jaw clenched. "Yes."

McAteer glanced at Caber, as if to say, *I told you this fellow was incompetent.* Then he went on with his examination.

"With the Nuyyad vessel destroyed," he told Picard, "you proceeded to a world called Magnia—Serenity Santana's home planet. Why did you not simply return to our galaxy?"

"The *Stargazer* was in desperate need of repairs," the captain explained. "Had we attempted to cross the barrier, I would have exposed my crew to the energies that transformed Gary Mitchell some seventy years ago."

"I see," said McAteer. "That sounds like a legitimate concern. But why Magnia?"

"It seemed like our best chance to get parts we could use. If the Magnians originally came from Earth, there were bound to be certain similarities between their technology and our own."

"Under the circumstances, a reasonable assumption," the admiral allowed. "But when you arrived at Magnia, there was a ship in orbit. A Nuyyad ship, as I understand it."

"Indeed," said Picard. "A reminder to the Magnians that they were at the mercy of the Nuyyad."

"You heard that later," said McAteer, "if I recall the substance of your logs, and never received any confirmation of it. But for now, let us deal with your decision to attack *this* Nuyyad vessel as well. I don't suppose you made any attempt at contact in this instance either?"

"I did not," Picard told him. "I had already seen the behavior of her sister ship. And had I contacted her, it would have allowed her to prepare for our confrontation—which would have sealed our fate, considering our shield emitters and weapons batteries were still barely operational."

McAteer looked incredulous. "So you attacked a vessel that made no aggressive action toward you?"

It sounded so absurd when expressed in those terms. But Picard had known he was right to attack that ship.

"I followed my instincts," he said.

McAteer affected a sad smile. "Instincts are fallible. That is why Starfleet has protocols and regulations—which you, apparently, chose to ignore."

"I did not ignore them," said Picard. "I considered them and decided they did not apply."

"In your judgment," said McAteer.

"That is correct," said the captain.

"The same judgment that led you to trust Serenity Santana?" The admiral chuckled derisively. "Isn't it true that by this time you suspected Miss Santana of treachery—of leading you and the *Stargazer* into a trap orchestrated by the Nuyyad?"

"It is," Picard had to concede.

"But in your *judgment,* it was advisable to engage the Nuyyad a second time?"

The captain glanced at the other two admirals. Caber was regarding him sternly, no doubt with disapproval. Mehdi, on the other hand, seemed to be suffering, obviously unhappy with the way the questioning was going.

"It was," said Picard.

"I see," said McAteer. "And as I understand it, you weren't finished. Later on, after you had completed your repairs with the help of the Magnians, you could have recrossed the barrier without worrying about your crew's exposure. Yet you chose a different course. You went after a Nuyyad supply depot."

Picard frowned. "Starfleet sent me across the barrier to see if there was any truth to the reports we had received about the Nuyyad. I was satisfied that they were indeed a threat to us—that, in fact, they were in the midst of preparing an invasion."

"But in your own words, Starfleet had sent you across the barrier to see if there was any truth to those reports. Did Starfleet also ask you to make a tactical strike against the Nuyyad?"

"It was not what I had been ordered to do," Picard confirmed. "However, as a Starfleet captain, I am charged with the security and defense of the Federation, and in that light I believed this action was both necessary and justified."

"Justified by what? The word of people who had already proven themselves untrustworthy?"

The captain felt a hot spurt of anger. McAteer had no idea what it was like on the other side of the barrier. He had no right to level such a criticism.

No, he thought, remembering his oath. *As your superior, he has every right.*

"By that time," he said, "I was inclined to believe the Magnians' story. First, they had explained the reasons for their deception to my satisfaction. Second, after our destruction of the ship orbiting Magnia, the Nuyyad had reappeared in force and carried out a potentially devastating attack."

"I wonder," said McAteer, his voice dripping with sarcasm, "if what you did to their other ships had something to do with that."

"They did not attack *us*, Admiral. They attacked *Magnia*."

"If your logs are accurate," said McAteer, "a number of your people were on the planet's surface by then, working hand in hand with the Magnians. The Nuyyad must have perceived that and come to the only reasonable conclusion—that the one certain way to remove the threat posed by the *Stargazer* was to take control of Magnia and extract your personnel."

"Or," said Picard, "they were as vicious and grasping as the Magnians claimed."

"The point," said the admiral, stiffening a bit under the lash of the captain's retort, "is that you didn't *know*. You couldn't be certain. And yet you felt this was sufficient evidence to warrant an attack on a nonmilitary target."

"It was *not* nonmilitary," Picard maintained. "It was significantly better armed than the Nuyyad's *ships*."

"It was a *supply* depot," McAteer insisted. "It could have contained nothing more than foodstuffs."

"With all due respect," said the captain, "you helped foil an invasion fleet a few weeks ago by stowing aboard a supply ship. That contained foodstuffs as well."

The admiral took the point in stride. More than likely, he had considered it already and prepared a response.

"I was helping to defend the Federation against a documentably hostile fleet that had already invaded our space," said McAteer. "You, by contrast, were in alien space—the Nuyyad's, for all we know—which would have made *you* the invader. I don't believe our situations were at all the same."

"All I am saying," said Picard, "is that a supply facility may be a key component of an invasion fleet."

"And then again," the admiral insisted, "it may *not* be. Which is why we don't attack them unless and until we are certain. And the veracity of the Magnians notwithstanding, you were not in a position to be certain."

"Unfortunately," said Picard, "we are seldom in that position. A starship captain must be prepared to act on what information is at hand, no matter how scanty or unsubstantiated."

"Or *not* act," said McAteer, "as I believe you should have done in the case in question." He looked to his colleagues. "I have no further questions."

That meant it was Mehdi's turn. The captain relaxed a bit, knowing that *this* admiral wasn't out to take his job away. Quite the contrary.

"It's true," he began, "that Captain Picard acted on an incomplete knowledge of the facts—just as we are doing in judging him. But while we're considering the damage he may have done, let's also consider the good."

Inwardly, Picard cheered Mehdi on.

"If the captain was correct in his assessment of the Nuyyad," said the admiral, "he rescued a world full of human expatriates from a bloody oppressor. Then he went on to save the Federation and maybe this entire sector from war and the possibility of conquest. Not a bad thing, by any means."

"But it's far more likely," said McAteer, "that he created an unnecessarily hostile situation, and it falls to us to hold him accountable for that."

"If that's what he did," said Mehdi, "yes. Let's strip him of his command. But what if this hostile situation existed prior to Captain Picard's arrival on the scene?"

"There's no proof of that," McAteer noted. "Only the word of Santana and the other Magnians, and we have already established what that's worth."

Mehdi sighed out loud. "It would be nice if we could hear from someone who *hasn't* tried to deceive us. Someone who has lied to neither Captain Picard nor anyone else."

He stood there for a moment, apparently mourning the lack of such a witness. Then he walked to the back of the room, passing through the gallery, and pressed the stud in the wall that opened the door.

As it slid aside, it revealed someone standing in the corridor outside, flanked by security guards. He was tall and bulky, but he had tiny, dark eyes, and a fringe of lank hair encircling his otherwise hairless head.

Picard couldn't believe his eyes. It was *Dojjaron*.

Chapter Nineteen

SLOWLY AND DELIBERATELY, the foremost elder carried his bulk into the courtroom, followed by an armed security guard, looking neither right nor left at the officers in the gallery. It wasn't until he came within a couple of meters of the admirals' table that he stopped.

"I have come to speak," he said, as if that constituted a momentous event.

He looked every bit as self-assured as he had on the *Stargazer,* every bit as fierce and belligerent. He was only standing there, motionless except for the subtle flaring of his nostrils, but it was clear that he came from a martial culture.

The only new element in the Nuyyad's appearance was his choice of garb. Instead of the breastplate he had worn back on the ship, he was wearing a loose black and white robe, cinched at the waist with a black sash.

It spoke eloquently of formality—Dojjaron's sole acknowledgment of the solemnity of these proceedings.

McAteer went red in the face. Obviously, the admiral had paid enough attention to the *Stargazer*'s logs to recognize a Nuyyad when he saw one.

Mehdi, on the other hand, seemed approving as he returned to the front of the courtroom. Obviously, he had known about the foremost elder's entrance in advance, even if Picard hadn't. And now that the captain thought about it, Dojjaron could have attended the hearing only if someone vouched for him. It didn't seem likely that it had been McAteer.

As for Admiral Caber . . . he didn't seem to have any reaction at all to the alien's entrance. But that didn't mean he wasn't seething every bit as much as McAteer underneath that cool exterior.

"I protest," said McAteer, shooting to his feet.

Mehdi looked at him. "On what grounds?"

McAteer pointed to Dojjaron. "This individual has no business attending this proceeding."

"I disagree," said Mehdi. "You have charged Captain Picard with creating a hostile situation. It's our responsibility to examine the truth of that charge."

"But he's not a citizen of a Federation member world," McAteer pointed out.

"Since when," Mehdi wondered out loud, "is truth the exclusive province of the Federation?"

McAteer narrowed his eyes in frustration. "There's no precedent for this and you know it."

"There doesn't have to be," said Mehdi. "It's not a court-martial. It's just a hearing, remember?"

McAteer looked as if he wanted to launch another objection. But apparently, he had been outmaneuvered.

"Go ahead," he said weakly.

Mehdi turned to the Nuyyad. "Please understand," he said, "whatever you say in this room must be the truth. There's no room here for lies or misdirection."

"The concept has been explained to me," said the alien.

"All right, then. Your name?" Mehdi asked.

"I am called Dojjaron, Foremost Elder of the Nuyyad."

"Why are you here, Foremost Elder?"

"I have come to enlighten you and your fellow judges." He glanced at McAteer. "There seems to be a misconception as to what took place on the other side of the barrier, between your Captain Picard and the Nuyyad."

"A misconception?" said Mehdi. "In what way?"

"I have heard it said that Picard would have been wiser to leave us alone—that he made enemies of the Nuyyad when he could have avoided doing so."

Apparently, Dojjaron had been given closed-circuit access to the hearing. *Clever,* thought the captain.

"And this is inaccurate?" asked the admiral.

"Let there be no doubt—we had every intention of invading your galaxy. And we would certainly have done so except for the actions of your Captain Picard."

"Really," said Mehdi.

"Yes. Though his vessel must have sustained some

serious damage, he decided not to limp home. Instead, he went after a supply depot we had established, and destroyed it."

"And this decision—this action—had the effect of forestalling your invasion?"

"Yes," said Dojjaron. His eyes narrowed to dark points. "If only for the time being."

"So you still intend to invade us?"

The Nuyyad grunted. "It is only a matter of time."

"Thank you," said Mehdi. He turned to his colleagues. "Any further questions of the Foremost Elder?"

"I have a few," said McAteer. As he got to his feet, Mehdi sat down to give him the floor.

McAteer studied the alien for a moment. Then he said, "Tell me, what made you come here to speak on Picard's behalf?"

"I owe it to him," said the Nuyyad.

"You owe it to him," the admiral echoed for dramatic effect. "And why would that be, Foremost Elder? What did you receive from Picard that inspired such gratitude?"

"His cooperation in destroying Brakmaktin."

"Who was a threat to your people, I gather."

"He was, yes."

"So much so that you made a journey through the barrier to see him eliminated."

"That is true."

"So Picard did you a turn, and now you're doing him one."

Dojjaron lifted his chin. "As I said."

"And to what length," asked the admiral, "would you go to repay your friend Picard?"

"He is not my friend," said the Nuyyad. "He was my ally, but now he is nothing to me. As for what length I would go to . . . he did my people a great favor. There is little I would not do."

"Would you lie for him?" asked McAteer.

The Nuyyad's eyes screwed up. "Of course."

The admiral smiled. "And is that what you're doing now? Lying before this tribunal in order to save Picard's command?"

Dojjaron's lip curled. "Among my people, we have word-twisters too. We flay their skin from their bones and stake them out in the wastes, to be devoured by predators."

That gave McAteer pause, but only for a moment. "Answer the question," he insisted.

"Of course I would lie for Picard," said Dojjaron. "But in this instance, I am telling the truth. He saved you and your people from conquest. You should honor him instead of humiliating him."

The admiral's eyes sparkled. "That's for us to decide." He turned to Caber. "Anything, Admiral?"

Caber shook his head.

McAteer turned back to the Nuyyad. "Then you're excused."

Dojjaron stood there a second or two longer, as if to say he would leave whenever he felt like it. Then he made a sound of disdain and trundled out of the room, his security escort following dutifully in his wake.

McAteer took in his fellow admirals with a glance. "I, for one, have heard enough. Admiral Caber?"

"So have I," came the response.

McAteer turned to Mehdi. "Admiral?"

Mehdi didn't look eager to invite the next step, but he had no choice. "Of course." As he sat down, he exchanged looks with Picard. The captain smiled at him, grateful for all he had done.

Indeed, he had put up a good fight. In any other court, it would have made a difference. And by the same token, Dojjaron's testimony would have peppered the opposition's argument with holes a starship could sail through.

But this wasn't any other court. Picard's future as a captain in Starfleet lay solely in the laps of three men, one of whom happened to be his accuser.

In other words, he didn't stand a chance.

According to protocol, the admirals would present their verdicts one at a time. McAteer offered to go first.

Clasping his hands in front of him, he shot a look of regret at Picard—one he had probably practiced in front of a mirror. Then he said what everyone in the room expected him to say.

"This is a difficult decision for me," he began. "However, Captain Picard demonstrated a serious lack of judgment and a disregard for established protocols in a clear-cut first-contact situation. Regardless of the outcome, he fell short of Starfleet's expectations. And in the process, he endangered all of us.

"To allow him to repeat his mistake would be a most grievous error on our parts. We can make only one responsible choice—to demote him and reassign command of the *Stargazer.*"

Leaving his words hanging in the air, McAteer sat back in his seat. And Admiral Mehdi sat forward.

"Obviously," he said, "Captain Picard diverged from recommended behavior in his dealings with the Nuyyad. But as we have seen, he was right to do so. Foremost Elder Dojjaron said so himself, and who would know better than he?

"Admiral McAteer may say Captain Picard was lucky. I say he was following the sort of instincts that encouraged me to grant him his captaincy in the first place. We must allow him to keep on displaying those instincts where he belongs—in the center seat of the *Stargazer.*"

Then it was Caber's turn. Picard smiled to himself. It had been a good run while it lasted.

Caber sat there for a moment, looking solemn. Then he addressed the room.

"Admiral McAteer," he said, "is a man who obviously has the good of the fleet at heart. And he makes a cogent argument for relieving Captain Picard of his command."

Picard bit his lip to keep from protesting. McAteer and Caber may have thought he was a loose cannon, but he wasn't going to do anything to confirm their opinion.

"As the admiral has said," Caber continued, "the evidence is clear. Captain Picard relied on the word of a woman who had already proven herself capable of lying to him."

It will not be so bad serving as a first officer, Picard thought. Or would they break him down even further?

"He diverged from Starfleet protocols, ignored his training, and resorted to violence in a first-contact situation."

Picard sighed. It had only been a few months since he was Captain Ruhalter's second officer. *I suppose I could live with that as well, if it comes to it.*

"I don't take the letter of Starfleet law lightly," Caber continued. "It represents the accumulated wisdom of a lot of intelligent men and women—the people who commanded starships before we were born. Some of them gave their lives furthering our knowledge of the universe."

But not on the Stargazer, Picard thought. That would be too much to ask. Walking the same corridors he had walked as captain, facing the same crewmen . . . except there would be pity in their eyes for what he had become. . . .

"And I'm not talking about survey data or navigation logs. I'm talking about how we approach a species we've never seen before—how we put our best foot forward, even when it places us in danger—because in the experience of all the captains who came before us, that's the way we get the job done."

Normally, thought Picard, *yes. But not in this case. It was too late for first-contact protocols.*

"I wish," said Caber, "that I could say I approved of the way Captain Picard handled the situation. However, I would have done it differently. And I, like

Admiral McAteer, believe that discrepancy is a direct result of Picard's inexperience."

The captain glanced at Admiral Mehdi, but he saw no hope there. Just a resignation that mirrored his own.

"As I see it," Caber declared, "Captain Picard's actions could have ignited a war between the Nuyyad and the Federation. It was only pure luck that those actions *prevented* a war instead."

McAteer looked as content as the captain had ever seen him. And why not? He had won.

"However," said Caber, "we need men who are lucky on the bridges of our ships, just as much as we need men who follow the letter of Starfleet law."

Picard wasn't certain that he had heard correctly. Was Caber actually saying something *good* about him?

"There's more than one way to skin a cat," said Caber. "And all those captains who came before us . . . they went with their gut reaction as often as they went with protocol, even though they were the ones who helped put the protocol in place.

"You can't teach instinct," he noted. "You can't imprint it. You can only give someone the leeway to make his own decisions and hope he shows some evidence of it—as Captain Picard did in his encounter with the Nuyyad."

I will be damned, Picard thought. *He is saying something good about me.*

"Admiral," said McAteer, protesting as the captain and Mehdi would not, "this is highly—"

"He may have been rash," said Caber, forging ahead despite his colleague. "He may have thrown caution to the winds. But let's not forget the fact that he was also *right*."

"To believe that," said McAteer, "you would have to take the word of a species we know nothing about." He glanced at the captain. "And thanks to Picard, we never will."

Caber appeared unimpressed. "Captain Picard may not have the ability to tell when someone's lying, Admiral, but I do. And Dojjaron was telling the truth. I'd stake my life on it."

"Then," said Admiral Mehdi, "you've decided to rule in Captain Picard's favor?"

"I have," said Caber.

McAteer turned crimson. "Admiral, you *heard* the evidence. I don't see how you can—"

"Maybe I'm wrong about him," said Caber. "Only time will tell, I suppose. But at this point, knowing what I know of him, I can't rule any other way."

McAteer looked as if he wanted to say more, to insist that his colleague see the matter as he did. But obviously, there was no point. Caber had made up his mind.

"Under the circumstances," said Mehdi, a smile of unexpected pleasure on his face, "I would have to say that Captain Picard has received a vote of confidence. I trust he will continue to prove deserving of it."

I will indeed, Picard thought.

At that juncture, McAteer probably wished he had chosen someone else for his jury, but it was too late. Having already extolled Caber's qualifications on the record, he could hardly contradict himself now.

Mehdi regarded McAteer. "Admiral?"

The muscles in McAteer's jaw worked furiously. But then, he had lost, and everyone knew it.

"The hearing is adjourned," he conceded, his voice flat and lifeless.

Mehdi turned to Picard. Considering his place on the jury, it would have been unseemly for him to pat the captain on the back. But the glance Mehdi shot him served the same purpose.

Moments later, Picard found himself out in the corridor, surrounded by several of his officers—Ben Zoma, Simenon, Greyhorse, Joseph, and the Asmunds.

"So you're still in charge?" asked Ben Zoma.

"It would appear so," said the captain, "yes."

Strange, he thought. He had been so certain that he would lose his command, so absolutely sure of it, it was difficult to come to terms with the fact that he hadn't.

"Just as well," Simenon responded. "I've begun to get accustomed to you."

The captain smiled at him. "And I you." He turned to Ben Zoma again. "Just one question—about Dojjaron."

"Amazing, isn't it? I didn't think he would spit on you if you were dying of thirst. But when he heard about the hearing, he insisted on testifying in your behalf."

"Then it was *his* idea?" Picard asked.

"His and no one else's," said Ben Zoma. "All I did was contact Admiral Mehdi, who—as you can imagine—was pleased as hell to have him as a witness."

"Speak of the devil," said Greyhorse.

Following the doctor's gaze, Picard saw Dojjaron lumber toward him. The Nuyyad still had his security escort.

Ben Zoma and the others stepped aside to let Dojjaron approach the captain. Had they not, they might have been crushed underfoot.

"Foremost Elder," said Picard, out of respect and gratitude.

"What was the outcome?" the Nuyyad asked.

"I will remain captain of the *Stargazer.*"

Dojjaron shrugged. "As you should." Then his expression hardened. "We will meet again, I believe. But it will not be in the spirit of cooperation and common purpose."

"You know," said the captain, "I believed I had no chance of keeping my command. And yet, I have. It gives me hope that other impossibilities will come to pass."

Picard was sure that Dojjaron understood what he was talking about. However, the Nuyyad didn't comment. He just grunted again and walked away.

It was then that the three admirals began to file out of the courtroom. Mehdi went first, looking like a load had been lifted from his shoulders. Next came McAteer, who somehow found the wherewithal to smile despite his defeat.

And finally, Caber. He had no particular expression on his face, offering no insight into how he felt about what had transpired.

"Excuse me," Picard told his colleagues.

Perhaps he should have let Caber walk away. But he couldn't. Not until he had satisfied his curiosity.

"Admiral?" he said, hurrying to catch up.

Caber stopped and turned to him. "Ah. Captain Picard."

"I would like to thank you for your vote of confidence, sir. I will do my best to prove worthy of it."

"I have no doubt of it," said Caber.

How can I put this? "I must say, sir, I was a trifle surprised . . ."

"Why is that?" asked the admiral.

"Considering what happened with your son . . . I thought you might hold it against me."

"Hold it against you?" Caber dismissed the idea with a flip of his hand. "Why would I do *that?* My son is a brat, Picard. And a bigot as well, judging from your report. And the only reason he'd gotten away with those shortcomings for so long is because his name is the same as mine."

"Then you . . . understand what I did?" asked Picard.

"Perfectly." A look of regret crossed his face like a passing shadow. "I just wish one of his other captains had had the nerve to do it first."

Picard didn't know what to say.

"If you'll excuse me," said Caber, "I have to get going. I'm glad everything worked out for you."

"Thank you," said the captain.

He watched the admiral vanish around a turn in the corridor. Then he smiled to himself and thought, *Remarkable.*

Epilogue

COLE PARIS LAY STRETCHED OUT on his bed, thinking.

Nikolas had moved back in with him, his request approved by Commander Ben Zoma. In fact, Nikolas would have been sleeping in his old bed at that very moment were it not for his restlessness.

It wasn't as bad as when he left the *Stargazer*, tortured by memories of Gerda Idun. However, he still had trouble sleeping, and he preferred a walk around the ship to any sedative Greyhorse might have prescribed for him.

Paris hadn't told Nikolas about Jiterica. At least, not yet. But he had confided in Nikolas weeks earlier, asking him what he thought of the possibility of a relationship between a human and a Nizhrak.

Nikolas had told him to go for it. And Paris was sure if he told Nikolas now how he had ruined that relationship with his jealousy, his roommate would have chided him for it.

After all, Nikolas knew how precious a lover could be.

Paris had been a fool, but he would be a fool no longer. Getting up from his bed, he pulled on his boots and his jacket and started for the exit, determined to make things right with Jiterica no matter what it took.

But before he reached the door, he heard the chime that told him someone was standing outside it. A little annoyed at the delay, he said, "Come in."

Then the door slid aside and Paris saw who was standing there, and his pulse pumped a little harder. "Jiterica," he said.

He had come to pride himself on his ability to decipher her expressions. But this time, he couldn't do it.

"May I come in?" she asked.

Paris didn't like the tone of Jiterica's voice. It was careful, guarded, as if she were doing her best to deal with him on a strictly unemotional level. And why would she do that—unless she intended to put an end to what they had?

"I need to tell you something," said Jiterica.

That sounded bad. People said things like that when they were breaking off relationships.

He didn't want to do that. Having had a taste of life with Jiterica, he couldn't imagine it without her.

"Listen," Paris told her, "you were right about my not liking Stave. I was jealous of him. But he's dead and I should have put your feelings ahead of mine and . . . I don't want to stop seeing you. I *can't*."

Jiterica stared at him from behind her faceplate. "Stop?" she echoed. "I don't want to stop. I just want to tell you that I forgive you."

Paris looked at her as if he had never heard the word before. "Forgive . . . ?"

Yes," she said. "And I hope you will forgive *me* for being so cold to you."

Paris had never been so happy to hear anything in his entire life.

Brakmaktin wasn't dead.

He didn't know it right away. In fact, he didn't know much of anything. Then, ever so slowly, his consciousness asserted itself, and he began to ascend. He escaped the embrace of the lava, the furnace that had melted his flesh and eaten his bones, and made his way into the calm, still precincts above it.

Were Brakmaktin still in possession of his eyes, he might have looked around and seen how empty his cavern was. Were he still in possession of his flesh, he might have felt anger as white hot as the pit.

And were he in possession of a throat, he might have scraped it raw with howls of frustration.

But Brakmaktin had none of these things. He was only an essence now, an awareness that he was different from all that was around him and had been even more different before his corporeal form was taken from him.

But his physical self would have fallen away from him anyway. That was the irony—and he could still appreciate irony—of the changes that had taken place in him when the barrier infused him with its power and majesty.

Brakmaktin had thought of it merely as energy, but it was infinitely more than that. It was life itself. Not the life he had lived when he was but a shell, but life as it could be, unfettered, unlimited, and exalted.

And now that he had been liberated from his flesh, he no longer yearned to multiply and continue his bloodline. It was difficult to remember why that had been of such importance to him.

But he still yearned—not as a parent, but as a child. For the barrier had given birth to him in its way, remaking him in its image, and his longing to return to it was more powerful than any sun in the vast, black void.

Rising effortlessly, Brakmaktin cleared the layers of rock above him and made his way through the atmosphere of the world he had tortured with his ambition. He might have been sorry if he were capable of sorrow, but that emotion had been denied him even before he touched the barrier.

As it was, he put his actions behind him, recognizing them as trivialities, and reached into the vacuum for the only thing in the universe that mattered to him.

He had been away, but he was going home.

Picard could have sent a communication via the ship's intercom. However, his shift on the bridge was over, and he preferred to deliver the message in person.

It didn't take long for the door to Serenity's quarters to slide aside, revealing their sole occupant. "Jean-Luc," she said.

"My navigator has located your vessel," he told her. "Barring the unforeseen, we will reach it in a few hours."

Shc absorbed the information. Then she said, "Come in."

As the door slid closed behind him, Serenity looked into his eyes. Hers, as always, were so beautiful it sent a chill through him.

This moment was hardly a surprise—they had both known it would come. But it bore a weight for which Picard wasn't really prepared, and he suspected that Serenity wasn't either.

"We've been here before," she said, "haven't we? Parting ways, saying good-bye?"

"We have," he agreed. "Except, as I recall, it was in a mountain meadow last time, with Magnia's sun turning the sky ablaze in the background."

Serenity looked around her quarters. "I guess you'd have to say this is a little different."

He nodded. "Decidedly."

"Last time," she said, "I asked you if you would miss me. You didn't quite say you would."

"Nor did I say I wouldn't."

Serenity smiled a little. "Not the decisive response one would expect from the commander of a Federation starship."

He held his hands out in an appeal for reason. "Even with everything that happened that day, I didn't know if I could trust you. You had already lied to me, and I had fallen for it. It was difficult to be certain of your motives after that."

"And this time?" she asked. "Do you feel it's necessary to question my motives?"

Picard smiled back. "This time you were completely trustworthy. At least, I believe you were. I have yet to see if you pilfered any of the towels."

That got a laugh out of her. "You know," she said, taking his hand, "I may have stolen any number of things. A thorough captain would demand a search of my person."

"Would he?" asked Picard.

"I'm sure of it." Her eyes danced with reflected light. "And he wouldn't trust a tricorder scan."

"Not if he were truly thorough, you mean."

"He would want to conduct the search himself. For the sake of security, of course."

"Of course," he said.

Then the captain kissed her. And that, as it turned out, was just the beginning.

Some time later, Picard heard Ben Zoma calling his name over the intercom system. "Yes?" he said.

"We've found the Magnians' ship."

The captain was sorry to hear it.

"And," Ben Zoma added, "the foremost elder is impatient to leave us."

I am sure he is. "Thank you, Gilaad. Picard out."

"I have to go," said Serenity, her head on his shoulder.

Picard brushed her raven hair off her face. "Yes. I know."

"Perhaps we'll see each other again *before* the safety of the galaxy demands it."

"I hope so," he said.

But of course, he couldn't say. After Picard's competency hearing was over, Admiral Mehdi had spoken to him about the possibility of a long-term mission—one that would take the *Stargazer* far from the attentions of Admiral McAteer, into the unexplored regions beyond the bounds of the Federation.

It was right up Picard's alley. But then, wasn't that what Starfleet was all about? Pushing the envelope? Going where no one had gone before?

"A new chapter for the *Stargazer*," Mehdi had called it. And the captain had liked the sound of it—almost as much as he liked the look in Serenity's dark brown eyes.

"I guess I should get ready," she said.

"Both of us," he told her.

Soon, he would be watching her vanish from his life again—perhaps forever. But then, he had thought the same thing when he left Magnia, and here he was holding Serenity in his arms again.

Forever is a very long time, Picard told himself. *Anything can happen.*

Anything.

Acknowledgments

If writing *Star Trek* books teaches you anything, it's that zipping through space is not a one-man job. Wherever you're headed, whether it's just around the block to Alpha Centauri or all the way out to the galactic barrier, you'd better surround yourself with good hands. Otherwise, you're space pizza.

This author has been privileged to have the best crew in the fleet. Margaret Clark, my editor on *Maker* and a slew of other books, has plied uncharted territory with a steady hand and a salty jape ever since we began working together more than a decade ago. Scott Shannon, my publisher, has kept the warp drive purring, the deflector shields up, and the phaser banks fully charged. And Paula Block of Viacom Licensing, blessed with the skill of a Starfleet surgeon, has extracted any number of troublesome plot points without leaving so much as a hairline scar.

And of course, there's the guy who started it all—Gene Roddenberry. The Zefram Cochrane of the *Star Trek* universe, Gene came up with the engine that still propels us through the void, eagerly seeking all those strange new worlds.

STAR TREK